PRESENTED BY HOT INK PRESS

NAUGHTY BEDTIME STORIES: SECOND CHANCES

A HIP Anthology

Naughty Bedtime Stories:

Second Chances

Published by Crushing Hearts and Black Butterfly Publishing

Copyright 2015 held by CHBB Publishing and the Individual Authors

Cover by Rue Volley
Edited by Olivia Harper

Dedicated to everyone who needs a second chance…

TABLE OF CONTENTS

MY MASTER BE

By: Aurelia Fray

One

"Cut!" he screams across the shitty back-lot set. Frankie Desire is the hottest music video producer in the world right now. The bands he has represented to date, read like a name-dropper's wet dream. He is hot—smoking fucking hot—in every sense of the word, but he is also a fucking dick and a miserable, sour-faced, overly-demanding shit.

We've been on set for the last eight hours without a break, trying to get a stupid shot of me dancing with a live tiger. Seriously, this thing looks set to eat me. Why wouldn't he? I am dressed like a seasoned steak. Daisy, from make-up, keeps running over to oil me up. Her hands curve over my backside one too many times and I just know she is getting a huge thrill out of touching my ass. Mind you, her hands are warm and my ass is freezing. I enjoy her touch just as much, although probably not in the same way.

"That okay for you, Gee?" Daisy asks, her eyes glittering up at me. She squats provocatively; her ass pushes out so I can see the ample curves jut out beyond her back as well as the bulge of her breasts, which are pressing against my leg. I nod in response. It is too cold to speak and, if you want the truth, I am a little afraid to open my mouth right now. I am so pissed off; I am liable to say something nasty. Daisy wouldn't deserve it, but the fool walking toward me in the spray on leather pants does.

"What is wrong? Hmmm? You got a problem with the tiger or your two left feet? You are supposed to be making this look sexy, Gee, not wobbling around like Jell-O on toothpicks."

"So, I am fat, can't dance and couldn't look sexy if I tried? You try dancing in these heels for eight hours straight. The tiger is pissed and hungry; the crew are pissed and hungry; the dancers are close to quitting, and I am ready to shove my foot so far up your ass that you'll be deep throating the nine inch heels you insisted I wear. You are an asshole, Frankie, and I think you know it!"

"Who do you think you are, talking to me like that? You think you are special, honey? You singers are a dime a dozen . . ."

"You think we have any less number of wannabe directors? I could pull any fucking asshole off the street in this neighbourhood and he could do a better job than you." I am yelling now and the bleary-eyed crew have stopped what they are doing to listen. Jenny Black, my sometimes manager—sometimes friend, looks ready to kill me. She hurries over. Her displeasure with me wrinkles her face like a prune. She shakes her head and waves her hands to stop me saying what she knows I am going to say. I can see her begging me, with her tired eyes, not to do it—not to waste this chance to work with one of the modern greats—but she is too late. I don't give a crap about how good he is, or how many people want to kiss his ass, or how many times Jenny had to suck him off for him to agree to work with us. No. I'd had enough.

"Do you know what," I smirk nastily. Jenny's eyes fly wide. Her lips form into a silent '*no*'. "I might do exactly that," I sneer.

"You think some random asshole can do what I do?" He laughs bitterly.

"Yeah, I think they could *and* they could probably do it better too. I mean, have you even listened to my track all the way through? Do you know the lyrics or the kinds of fans we have? Do you even give a shit about the message this song kicks out?"

"I don't need to understand it. I need to make you look good and, baby, we have been here *all fucking day* and you *still* don't look good."

"Fuck you, Frankie. Pack up your shit, take your fucking tiger and go. You're fired. Fucking asshole, quasi-lunatic bastard," I grumble. Jenny's complexion has changed to a funny shade of green and instead of standing beside me—demonstrating that she supports my decision—she runs after Frankie. I can hear her begging him to come back and finish the shoot, swearing that she will keep me in line. He says something about putting me on a leash. I laugh at that. Been there, done that and found most of my dates preferred to be the one on their knees.

"Jenny. You got ten seconds to figure it out or you'll be joining him," I call to her, as calmly as possible, across the lot. She glares at me but stomps back as she knows she should.

"What the hell are you thinking? You have no idea how hard it was to get Frankie Desire to agree to do this!" She snaps when she is close enough for me to see the veins popping out on her forehead.

"I have an idea—"

"No, you dirty bitch, it didn't involve my lips on his dick!"

I shrug my shoulders nonchalantly. Yeah, that's what I was thinking and nine times out of ten I'd have been right. "Oh God, the money we have already spent. *Shit!*" Jen stomps her foot, probably to stop herself hitting me.

I was oddly aware that everyone could still hear us and I, sure as shit, didn't want to have this conversation in front of the crew. Turning to the gawking crowd, I yell, "Shows over. Go home. Be at the studio conference room by ten AM on Sunday. You are all fucking booked for two weeks so we might as well do this thing ourselves." I was glad that Jenny suggested we hire all the crew and equipment ourselves instead of using Frankie's preferred team. Not only did it save us money, but also Frankie was famous for pulling tantrums and storming off for weeks at a time. Whenever he did, his crew stopped too and there had been many releases delayed until the dirty diva was satisfied. Jenny had to have known we would lose him at some point. Why else would she put in all the safety precautions?

"Oh, except you!" I yell at the animal trainer guy, "I'm not dancing with any fucking wild animal. Get paid for today and then fuck off."

"Gee!"

"What? I'm lucky I didn't get eaten by that giant pussy!"

"Wouldn't have been the first time –" Jen rebukes and finally cracks a smile.

"Shut the hell up. You enjoyed it and don't deny it. It's the only reason you're still my manager. Plus your pussy isn't *that* huge." I chuckle, pointing over to the prowling jungle cat. Jenny laughs and shakes her head. The smile, however, is quickly replaced by a sadness that I can't ignore.

"What are we going to do?" Her tone smacks of defeat. I have to suck in a breath to choke back the lump forming at my throat. I hate seeing her like this.

"Hire a new guy, someone really new and eager to please. Newbies are desperate to prove themselves. We just need to pick one with a shred of talent."

"I will trawl through our connections tonight see if we can't find someone." Jen nods. Her response lacks enthusiasm and I can feel the weight of her burden from where I stand. Perhaps I ought to get personally involved in the business side of things? Hiring and firing couldn't be too hard. At least if I stepped up, it might free Jen to get on with other things.

"Great. I will take a hand in this. Set up the interviews and make sure I'm there. I want to prove to that asshole that I was right." I try to sound upbeat and in control but it's not enough to pull Jen out of her mood.

"Not to mention, if you don't sell the new album, we lose the studio, the label and everything with it," she adds. I bite my lip and try to think of the right response.

We started up our recording label after Forrester, my previous label, changed my contract for the third time in two years. Each time I worked harder and earned less for my efforts. Jenny talked me into leaving and starting up our own label. It was a great idea except for the fact that I was working my panties off just to keep the bills at bay. We needed to sign a few more bands because my niche metalcore following couldn't keep us afloat. I needed to break it big with this next album or we were going to have to walk away from the whole enterprise. Our desperation to be noticed was probably why we hired Desire-the-Douche in the first place.

"I know. I promised you we would make this work," I respond.

"But if the new album tanks—" She groans and shakes her head.

"We're fucked," I finish for her.

"Totally."

Two

"Well thank you for your time," Jenny says politely to a teenager in a three-piece suit. He is fresh out of art school replete with certificate, boundless enthusiasm, and empty resume. He knows he doesn't have the job. The fact that I popped gum the whole way through his interview probably tipped him off. It's not like his work wasn't great. It was. It was really good in a surreal, light-show kind of way. It was more about *him* not being right. He turned up to the interview in a suit for fuck sake. He had probably never listened to anything harder than classic rock.

"That's the seventh one today. I think we should face the music," Jen sighs.

"Ha, fucking, ha ha."

"Seriously, Gee. We just won't find someone in time. We should cancel the crews and pray we only lose our deposit and not the whole two week sum."

"Just wait. Have we got more to see?" I ask, an idea forming in my mind.

"Three more out there and one due to arrive any minute."

"Okay." I stand up and make my way to the double-wide corridor where our potentials are waiting. This one by one interview thing is annoying, not to mention it takes too long.

"Hey!" I wave at them. Two guys and a girl look up. One of them recognises me the other two look confused. "Okay, you and you can go, I say decisively and see Jenny hit her head against the wall from the corner of my eye.

"You," I say to the remaining twenty-something male. "You got any ink?"

"No." Not a good response but he was young. Plus, it wasn't really a prerequisite I was just curious. I tried another question.

"Heard of *Gravitas Chains*?" I ask. The band was a little mainstream but anyone who knew metal and metalcore would have heard of them.

"Sure."

"What's your favourite track of theirs?"

"*Weeping Ash* is pretty good." He responds looking a little more confident. He has finally clicked that the interview has begun. That song was pretty well known. I ask him one more question before I agree to chat with him further.

"What did you think of their *Primitive* album?"

"They don't have an album called *Primitive*. Not that I've heard about at any rate." And, *dingdingding,* we have a winner.

"Okay, go through to the office." I turn to Jenny with a grin. "Hey, at least he knows his music! Better than some of the others so far this morning." Jen shakes her head and follows the guy into the room. He interviews well and he knows his music, he is looking good, even if his cinematography is a little more novice than amateur. Truth is, he is the best we've seen all day and I'm desperate enough to give Jenny the head nod that will hire him. Just as I lift my chin, the door bursts open and in walks a fucking dream.

Tall, wiry- athletic build, defined arms and torso—and yeah I can tell, because he's wearing a tee that shows off all of those chiseled lines. His arms are a canvas filled with layered images that I could spend all day perusing and his ebony hair is up in one of those top knots that have become fashionable in recent months. I want to know how long it is when he lets it down, but I clamp my mouth shut before I say something stupid.

"Are you done yet?" he asks. Jenny glares in his direction. She looks set to tear into him when he grins, flashing a pretty line of straight pearly whites. *Fuck! He is amazing when he smiles.* Something tugs at my mind, a sense of familiarity but surely, if I had met this man before, I would have remembered. He isn't easily forgettable.

"I mean, am I too late for the interview? You guys have been in here ages and I don't want to waste my time outside waiting, if you've already hired."

I love his attitude. He sounds like me. He is me with a dick and balls and hot tattoos, a stunning smile, a day's beard growth and bright blue eyes. No wait, he isn't me. He is hotter than me. That little nugget brings me back to my senses.

"We were just finishing up. Perhaps you'd like to wait outside?" Jenny informs him. She is biting her lip. She wants to cuss him out for his rudeness but not in front of the potential director still sitting in front of us.

13

"Yeah well, before you hire Snowflake here, perhaps you want to look at this." He launches a USB drive across the conference table. It skids to a halt right at my hand. As soon as my fingers reach around the little rectangle of plastic, he walks out of the room allowing the door to swing shut behind him. I incline my head. My eyebrows dance and Jenny shakes her head in frustration.

"Mr. Frost, we are impressed by you but, in the interest of fairness, we will finish all the interviews and then contact the most suitable candidate. Please keep your week free until you have heard from us," Jenny singsongs, showing Snowflake the door. I wondered how the next guy knew Frost's name? Snowflake exits and Jenny spins on her delicate heels to face me.

"Put his stick in your slot already," she grumbles, "I know you are dying to." I can't stop my laughter. She knows me too well. The folder opens on my laptop and two files stare me in the face. The first titled 'watch me' and the second entitled 'watch you.'

I watch him first, then me. Clever bastard has done his homework. The first short film is about thirty seconds long. Just enough to whet my appetite. It is a visual resume of sorts and it blows me away. Watching it has me wanting to hire him, but it's the other video that has me wanting to fuck him.

He had picked a song off my last album. The song I liked most and had fought to get on the damn track list. The label wanted to dump it but I threatened to walk and instead they compromised by making it a secret track on the foreign export disks. Just knowing the song existed went in his favour. To this he edited together a montage

14

of soft focus clips, showing what appeared to be my body in sweaty positions with someone who looked very much like him. It was like watching myself perform highly artistic, black and white porn. Never do you see nipples, cock or cunt but the sinuous movement and rhythmic writhing has me wet. Everything about it speaks the song to the observer. He blurs the model's face, in a subtle *not-the-focal-point* way that I love. The camera follows the woman's hands as they move all over her body and his.

Jenny and I stare at each other in silence for a second or two before she whispers, "Wow."

"Yeah."

"No really. Fucking *wow*. That is sexy hot."

"It is."

"Want me to call him in or…"

"Or?"

"Do you, er, want a minute?"

"Just hire his ass before he leaves the building. Tell him to be here tomorrow morning. We need to work on a plan before the Sunday meeting. Oh and give him the track. Tell him to listen to it until he knows it backwards," I instruct. Jen grins and dashes outside. I can't face him and stay professional after that. I don't need a minute; I need a cold shower.

Three

Sunday morning rolls around and I find myself feeling nervous. I hadn't felt like this since the agent from Forrester appeared in Dougie's bar to hear me sing. I can still recall the way my legs shook as I took to the stage. I had a loyal following, even then, who had cheered and screamed along to my lyrics. Their enthusiasm for my sound got me through it. I needed a room full of them now.

Jenny volunteers to make calls whilst I debrief Mr. Hot-Stuff-Director. We are chasing a new band from the south and, just this morning, a friend warned us the band were doing the bar rounds in a desperate bid to get noticed. We also got a heads-up that my ex-label is after them too. The news only makes Jen even more determined to sign them with us.

The one-on-one with Hot-Stuff is probably the reason for my nerves. I wonder whether he will think me a diva for having such a heavy hand in his creative process or whether he realises that I own the lion's share of this new label. I didn't wonder for long.

Just like his interview, he walks in without knocking. He flings himself down into a chair across from me and, with a solid grunt, he moans, "No coffee? I don't function without coffee this early on a Sunday."

"On the counter. Get it yourself."

"Nice people skills you got there," he grumbles.

"Who's the girl?" I question him. I hadn't meant to but it had bugged me all night. The idea of him slicked-up and sliding with some wannabe me made me angry. Stupid, I know, but she shouldn't exist. There was only room for one me in this life.

"What girl?" He spins his head around to see who I'm talking about. When he realises we are definitely alone, he pours the tar-black Joe into a small cup and sits his fine ass back down. He stares straight into my eyes and responds to my question.

"Random model. She was the best I could get on short notice. Nothing like you in looks, which is partly why I kept a soft focus. Did you like it?" he asks. I shrug, answering his question with one of my own.

"Was okay. Did you listen to the track?"

"Yeah."

"What did you think?"

He shrugs. "Was okay," he replies with a dark grin. He leans across the table, his forearms tight and lean, his fists clenched. His eyes never leave mine. He smiles wider, enjoying the way I watch him. "Listen, I can play disinterested all day but we both know we are just wasting time. I know you liked my work or I wouldn't be sitting here. You know I like yours, baby, or I wouldn't be fucking sitting here. So let's not waste time screwing with each other. I know you want to see what I've got for you. For what it's worth, I think you are going to eat it up."

17

Holy fuck. He was saying all the right things for all the wrong reasons. *Shit.*

"Sure, tell me your ideas." I exhale on a stumbling breath.

"It's Xadian by the way."

"Hmm?"

"My name. Xadian or Xade, if you want to be lazy about it."

He gets up and strides purposefully towards me. His dark jeans are well worn. The black t-shirt, looser than yesterday's, has a band logo on it that I do not recognise. This close to me, I can smell his cologne. It fills my lungs like air, sweet and musky and male. I take a deep breath, pulling him deep into me and try not to react as he sits in the chair next to mine.

"Here," he whispers against my cheek, leaning in to hit the play button on the laptop. The intro to the single fills the room followed by my voice drawling out the first line.

The lyrics wrap around us and the screen dims to a hazy red. Lips move on screen, synching to my lyrics—thick, pouty, red lips— Kissable lips. Xadian speaks over the playback.

"You sing about vulnerability, but your videos sell sex, power and control. There is a disconnection between your songs and your image. So we need to do something about that."

I watch him watch the screen. Those hypnotic lips and nothing else fill our sight. No gimmicks, no scantily clad women, no chained up men or wild animals. Xadian closes his eyes, breathing in to the rise and fall of the harmony as my boy Keller shreds his guitar.

"This bit…" he says and then does something so fucking sexy. He sings my words back to me and I swear I'm going to come in my lace boy shorts. If I do, I might give them to him as a trophy. It would be the first time—since I was a teen—that a guy made me lose my shit without touching me.

"That, right there, is what we are going to hang the concept on," he says out of nowhere, forcing me to think about the lyrics because I am way too focused on his deep, fluid voice.

Lean in. Lean in.

Drink me up, take me in.

I wanna feel you on me.

Feel you on me, baby, taking over.

Master of me.

My Master be.

"You don't think that's about sex?" I ask him. It pretty much screams sex, power and control to me but, if he thinks otherwise, I would hear him out.

"You are asking to be taken care of: protected and loved unconditionally." His reading of my lyrics makes me feel a little nervous. He is stripping the song bare and I know he is right, but I wonder how he is able to see through it so easily.

"Strange, because I thought that I was asking to be fucked by a man who knew what the hell he was doing." I shrug, trying to lighten the seriousness of his mood. Xadian just stares at me. His eyes are kind but unforgiving too. He sees through me, through my lyrics and isn't going to sit and listen to my shit. "Okay, so say we go with your lovey-dovey shit. What then?" I speak to break the tension his scrutiny evokes but he doesn't let it slide.

He snorts. "You think being taken care of, adored, worshiped and protected is lovey-dovey shit?"

"It's not fucking."

"No, you're right, it's not. It's better," he informs me with that shit-eating grin. I want to tell him *I wouldn't know* but I'd be admitting to never having had someone respect me enough for sex to mean something more than sweaty rutting. Don't get me wrong, I loved my nasty sex, I just had nothing more meaningful to compare it to. I honestly believed sex with feelings was just a fictional concept made up to sell books, movies, and sentimental pop songs by ex-Disney princesses.

Xadian observes my reaction to his words and, from the way his eyebrows raise in surprise, I can see I might as well have spoken my thoughts aloud because the smug bastard has just read them in my face anyway.

"Never?" he asks. I shake my head and bite my lip. The unconscious gesture does something to Xadian though. He becomes distracted. His chin lifts slightly, his lips pout and his pink tongue darts out to lick the lower lip.

Shit, that is sexy.

"I can see I'm going to have to convince you that I am right," he declares without looking away from me. His eyes darken even as I gaze at him, he rolls his shoulders as though readying for battle.

Yum. Wait. What were we talking about again?

"The video!" I say aloud, answering my own damn question.

"Yeah. I'm going to pitch my idea to you, but I need you to do as I say. Do you think you can handle that, Gee?" His hand reaches out and strokes my cheek. I should slap it away or make a snide comment or something, but I just nod because his touch feels so good.

"Sure," I whisper as my eyes close. I intend to blink, to rest my lids a second and break the intense connection of his stare, however my eyes stay closed and I focus on the barely-there nature of his sensual voice.

"Let's take off your jacket. I need you to be comfortable," he mutters, sweeping the cropped leather garment from my shoulders. "Up on the table," he demands. Normally pushy men rile me. I don't often let people tell me what to do, Desire-the-Douche is a prime example of this. I can only take it for so long before my nature kicks in and I mouth off. Yet, Xadian is different. He intrigues me and instead of putting him in his place, I go with it. I want to see what he plans to show me. He thrills me.

I boost myself onto the desk. The wood feels cold against my black skinny jeans but I ignore it. I have a feeling I might be warming up soon, especially if he carries on staring like he can't get enough of me. I stare back. Unexpectedly, there, in the heat burning in his eyes, and the slight twist at the corner of his lips, is that sense of familiarity again. Is he setting off the spidey-senses or is it just that this man makes me horny? Who can fucking tell? The tingles he arouses within me are pretty much in the same place anyway. I keep my mouth shut and cocked into a perfect cheeky smile. I wait for his next instruction and try not to breathe too raggedly.

"Slide back. That's it. Good girl." *God that sounds hotter than I would have imagined.* His praise splits my smile a little wider, my eyes cut away in a nervous excitement. "Lean back until your back is flat against the wood. Yeah, that's it. Now get yourself comfortable and relax. I want you to close your eyes whilst I set up."

He leaves the room but is back in minutes with a camera on a tripod. It is not serious kit in the slightest. He sets it up at the far end of the room. I estimate that it will capture my shoulders to hips in its narrow range. At the opposite side of the room, he places two chairs. One blocks the door and the other sits just off-centre of the camera's focus, keeping him in shot throughout. On this chair he places a mini tripod and his smart phone. I wonder if he is trying to make a point about skill over equipment and then I realise that I don't care. This is just a trial run. Just the pitch.

While he sets up and fiddles with the focus on both cameras, I do as he requested and make myself more comfortable. I pull my hair out from underneath my body and lift it away so that I won't tug it out with any sharp movements. Shit like that hurts and I don't want to be screaming like an idiot if I can avoid it. Xadian looks over as I fumble with my hair.

"Take it out of the elastic," he instructs as he sits in his chair. I scoot up and pull my long blond hair up and over my shoulder. I unwind the elastic that holds it neatly back and I want to protest. It looks like shit and needs the gifted hands of a stylist, but he gazes at me in a way that says, "don't speak," so I don't. I don't say a word.

"Lay back, baby."

I lift my hair and hang it over the side of the desk. My shoulders are against the wood surface. I wait. The music starts again from somewhere in the room. For some reason it feels slower, moodier, than before. I like it.

"Run your left hand over your hair," he directs. "Stroke the side of your face with the tips of your fingers and then bring them down to the hollow of your neck." I do this and feel a current of electricity flowing through my fingers and into my flesh. Goosebumps rise up wherever I touch. I fight a shiver. I feel powerful and vulnerable all at once and it's driving me wild.

"Lower now. Trace every curve, baby. I want you to feel wherever the music takes you."

As alive as I feel from his words, and the tingling touch of my own fingertips, a cold slither of ice slips down my spine. Reality creeps around the illusion he is trying to create. I am too aware that this is my office, too aware of the camera on me, of the stranger directing me. My movements become stilted and unsure.

Just as I am about to tell him to stop, he shocks the shit out of me. Xadian stands between my legs and pulls them apart. I am still fully clothed and shouldn't be feeling the flush of heat or embarrassment of being exposed to him in this way. I mean, fuck. I'm not even exposed, but he is there, between my legs, and so fucking close to my pussy, covered or not, that I feel sure he will sense my desire. His large hands grip my upper thighs. The power of his grasp sears me through the material. His thumbs are so close to brushing the seams of my jeans where both legs meet at the crotch. He leans over so that I am witness to the intensity in his eyes.

"Relax. Let me show you." He takes my hand. Releasing my left thigh, he presses his fingers between mine until it looks like I've sprouted octopus fingers, and then caresses me with my own hand. It feels crazy good. His other hand comes into play and follows the path up and around my body. I suddenly want to be naked. I know that his touch, *our touch*, will burn me. Our hands slide up, slip down, grab, pinch, pull, squeeze, and stroke with abandon. No zone is forbidden and every touch is like fire.

I love it.

Then he lets go and returns to his chair. He restarts the track and I'm instantly reminded of why we are here; of what this is really all about.

"Gee!" he warns. I try to hold onto the feelings he provokes within my body. His soothing voice, calling out commands, eases me. I listen to him.

"Stroke your neck. Use your palms to push up those beautiful tits, baby. Lift your back, arch up as if you are reaching for me. Push both hands down your body, all the way until they are between your legs. Oh yeah, that's it. Now slow it down and look at me. Slow it all the way down until your hands stop over your heart. Great. Now face your head this way. Your eyes on mine, tell me with only your eyes, Gee, tell me everything you want from me."

And I do.

In that instant, my mind screams out through my eyes, begging him to hear me. The words, I yell, shock me.

Hold me. Want me. Caress me. Protect me. Guide me. Shield me. Love me.

Xadian stands up. He clicks off the camera phone and then strides purposefully towards the tripod and switches off the other device too. I try to sit up and pull myself off the table. Before I can, he is there between my thighs again. His face leans into mine.

"I heard you," he says, his voice a rough whisper, "I fucking heard you, baby."

I feel an unfamiliar and unwanted tingling at the corners of my eyes. The warning of impending tears surprises me. I haven't cried in years. I spent far too much of my childhood, shrivelled in one corner or another, weeping my guts out. As soon as I ran away from my dull-ass life, my overbearing mother and the asshole who liked to remind me that I would never be more than shit on his shoes, I made a promise to never let anything in—never feel deeply enough for it to hurt.

I was all cried out.

Gigi Shade was not the weak little girl that Regina Mallory had once been. Reinventing myself had cemented my own personal strength. Regina might have needed comfort but Gigi would take whatever she wanted. I stripped away the worst of me and left only the strongest parts standing and it worked too. I was hot, talented, driven and I was going to be happy. Someday soon it was all going to pull together and I would be happy.

Yet, here I am and I swear I am about to cry. Not because of some fucked-up lovey bullshit between us, just because of everything. Because of the shock at my own silent prayers, the humiliation of laying myself so bare, of the stupidity I feel at believing him and of the hope I have bubbling up inside that really *really* wants him to have heard me. I barely know this man and I want him to look after me. Whatever we're paying him is not nearly enough, if he has me believing my own bullshit.

Before these thoughts have time to twist into a sharp comeback. Before my tears even have time to wet my lashes, Xadian leans down and presses his mouth to mine.

His kiss is electric.

I feel it right down to my tingling toes. His hand reaches behind my head and pulls me into him. The kiss intensifies. His tongue meets mine, claiming dominance. My inner bitch has come to heel for this man and I have no idea why. Gently, and without breaking the union of our lips, he tugs me to my feet where I, unsteadily, lean into him.

"I want you," he admits and the words undo me. I don't need to answer, I am already unbuckling the big, black leather belt at his waist in a desperate bid to free him from these stupid jeans. I think I might have hummed something close to "*about fucking time*" but I can't be sure.

His mouth is on my throat. I franticly pull and yank at his clothes as he slowly, gently, teasingly nibbles at the spot behind my ear. I hear him chuckle when I grumble, "Fucking jeans are glued on!" He removes my hands before easily opening the buttons. His firm cock springs out and into my eager grip. I am only too happy to grasp him. I feel him, quantify him in my mind and am not disappointed. He laughs when I lick my hand, slicking it up, before reaching down and sliding it up and down his dick in a firm fist. He pulls off the layers of ripped vests and tees that I am wearing and traces the satin of my neon-pink bra. His fingertips are so calloused and rough that I can feel them on my skin, through the fabric.

My nipples sting. I am so turned on, it fucking hurts. He relieves them by pulling the fabric down and capturing one, then the other, with his mouth. My free hand grasps at his cheek, pulling him away when the suckling and nibbling sensations become too much. His mouth doesn't stay empty for long though. The instant I pull him away from my breasts, he takes my mouth again.

"This isn't what I meant to happen," he alleges between frantic kisses, "I intended to show you more."

"Show me more later, Xadian, right now this is all I need," I answer. He nods against my face, his stubble rubbing across my cheek as he fuses himself to me. I love the skin-to-skin thing. I love the way he melds into my flesh as if he is trying to crawl inside me—like he isn't complete without me.

"It is a promise then. More later, for now I'm going to fuck you up against this wall and hear you curse as you come. Sound

27

good?" He growls, spins me around and presses me to the wall. He moves so fast, I am not sure how he manages it, but he has me tight to the wall. His left hand clutches my neck, his long fingers extend up into my hair. He places enough force to keep my face against the cool brickwork as he glues himself to my back. My breasts are compressed; they pool out in excess either side of me. His right hand reaches down, a warm finger tracing a bulging boob, then skilfully removes what little clothing I am still wearing. I can feel his stiff cock against my searing hot skin. He pushes, grinding it against my ass as he whispers at my ear.

"No games. No foreplay. No time wasting, baby. Tell me you are ready to take me."

"I'm so fucking ready."

"Good girl."

His right hand slides down to rest flat across my aching mound and then he tugs, slides, part lifts me backwards in one skilful motion that has my backside jutting out in invitation and my back arched in readiness.

"Hands on the wall above your head. Use them to brace yourself off the wall when it gets too rough."

Holy fuck. When not if.

I fucking loved this man. I was feeling all kinds of crazy right now. Not just hot, or excited, or horny but commanded and desired. I was still as much in control. I gave him my trust, gave him the control he exuded over me and I could take it away at any point.

He is between my legs, his knee nudges them apart. The coarse fabric of his trousers scratches against my sensitive flesh. I glance backward to be sure and yeah, he has only pulled his pants down enough to screw me without friction burns or restriction. I don't know why, but the immediacy of his desire—the fact that he doesn't want to waste the time he could spend fucking me up the wall, by pulling down his trousers—turns me on even more. His desire fuels mine.

He keeps that one hand pressed against my mound, whilst he slides his rock hard dick up and down my dripping channel. He slicks himself up in my wetness and without hesitation presses the swollen tip against my tight opening. I am breathing heavily, anticipating the sting of his entry. There is nothing better than the stretching sting of a firm cock slipping inside.

As he penetrates I feel it, but not where I expect it. Xadian attempts to distract me from the burn by pinching my engorged clit and *boy* does it work. The acute pleasure-pain has me reeling. My head doesn't know which pleasure to focus on. He spins his fingers around in teasing circles upon the nub and then slides them between my lips, spreading them fully to the cool air ricocheting off my pussy with each of his smooth slides. He leans back and watches himself pump slowly inside me. *In and out. In and out.* I love the way he hums his desire. The sound is deep and reverberates at the back of his throat. It sounds like indulgence and pleasure.

He likes what he sees.

The hand at my clit slides up my abdomen and slips under my breast. He palms then grips firmly. His other hand, which has been clutching the back of my neck, glides down to grip the other breast. He slams into me. His heavy sac strikes repeatedly against my clit. His pelvis crashes against my ass. I am moaning and yowling like that fucking tiger from the other day.

"Put your weight into your arms, baby. Push back against me."

I do as he asks and I am rewarded with the glance of his teeth across my back. That sets me off. I am fucking coming all over him and he doesn't even slow down. In fact, he speeds up and gives me what he promised me. My legs and arms have turned to mush and I stumble against the wall. My whole body is pinned up by Xadian. He pumps hard, in strong upward motions, and every single thrust hits some magic place inside until I feel ready to come again.

He notices this time.

He sees the tremors take over my body as I buck and twist. He spins us around so that his back is to the wall, but slings one arm over my stomach to hold me up, whilst the other grips my throat firmly, yet gently, keeping our faces pressed together—side to side. I feel my eyes swim backwards. My mouth opens forming a silent *O*. My breath stop-starts and stutters. "Feel me, baby," he says as he thrusts once more and comes hard. We are both jerking, shaking, sweating. We collapse across the desk. He remains inside me for a few more, intimate, seconds and then carefully rolls away so that he is sitting on the chair at my back. I try to stand up, knowing he has a crude view of my pussy and the sticky-sweet evidence of our cheeky fuck.

"Your pussy looks pretty dripping with my cum," he says contentedly as if he had heard my thoughts. "I could sit here and stare at that all day, but I don't think your legs will hold out. Wait here for me." Xadian exits quickly and I, rather sullenly, grab for the clothes strewn haphazardly around me. I know that what happened was inevitable. The guy turns me on more than anyone I have ever met. The problem now, is seeing whether or not we can maintain a professional distance for the remainder of the project. The last thing I need is some stranger—even if he is a seriously hot fuck—thinking he can get away with murder because he has screwed me.

The door opens and I spin with the clothes in my hand. I hold them in front of me to protect my nakedness, but it's just Xadian. He looks pointedly at the clothes and quirks a solo brow at me. I drop them and face him boldly.

"Here you go," he reaches out for my hand. I stare at his open palm for a second, not sure whether or not to take it.

"Don't leave me cold, baby. I have something for you." Tentatively, I place my hand in his and permit him to sweep me across the space separating us. I am in his arms, then hoisted up so that my legs wrap around his waist. He moves like a dancer, sinuous and elegant, but he looks like a fallen angel—dark and delicious. A cold, damp swipe at my pussy tells me he has cleaned the evidence of our fucking away. He is the first lover to be considerate of me.

Usually they roll over and pass out, or I tell them to get dressed and fuck off. The gesture is somehow too intimate—too considerate.

"Gee. Listen…"

His words are slow and deliberate and I know what he is going to say. I have heard it before—shit, I have said the lines so many times myself that I know them backwards. I attempt to cut him off, raising my finger to his lips and plastering on a fake *okay baby, that meant nothing to me either* look on my face. I even manage the twinkle in my eye that tells him *I loved it, but no strings*. What I do not expect is for Xade's brows to furrow in annoyance.

"Now, hang on—"

"There's no need," I retort sharply. Pulling myself out of his grasp and sitting on the desktop. I fold my arms across my chest. He grimaces at both the literal and metaphorical distance I have created between us.

"I made you a promise, Gee. I always keep my word. There will be more, a lot more. I am going to show you what you've been missing," he insists, but I am not buying it.

"We both know that this was just—"

"Say another word and I swear I will put you over my knee!" Xade growls at me. He spreads his legs apart and braces himself to tackle me. The way he rounds his shoulders and flexes his fingers has me believing him. The fact that he means it gives me a delicious thrill. I almost open my mouth to provoke a spanking but he stoppers any words I might have said, with his thick tongue. He licks at the inside of my mouth and then pulls away with a satisfied grin.

32

"Just listen, okay?" I nod slowly, knowing that opening my mouth to speak will just be another invitation to kiss me.

"I have something to tell you that I think would be safer to say now before we go any further." The seriousness of his expression, combined with the dark choice of wording, twists within my gut, whatever he is going to say will be unpleasant.

I scoot to the edge of the desk, planting my feet firmly on the floor as if that might somehow help me to handle whatever he is about to confess. His hand reaches for my neck. My mind flashes hot images of him gripping me there whilst he hammered into me. I want him again. As stupid as it sounds I know it's true. I want more, just like he promised. If he told me to climb on the desk and spread wide, I would do it before he could finish speaking the words.

I have to take this seriously. The renewed sexual tension is clouding my thoughts. His wry smile turns to a frown and he watches my tormented expressions. He reads me wrong. He mistakes my resolve for aversion and barks angrily at me.

"You, Regina Mallory, are something fucking else," he proclaimed, shaking his head in disbelief. His use of my full name is like a bucket of ice-cold water, dousing whatever lusty flame flickered in my groin.

"What did you just call me?" I snap.

Awareness is a slow bitch. She flashes like a bright light in your mind, alerting you to the momentousness of discovery. However, that same flash blinds you—causes you to stumble— delays your reaction until the facts flood in and form a complete picture of truth in your mind. It takes too long for me to see that my instincts about Xade were correct, but by mentioning my name—the name that no one, save my family, knew—my awareness flashed.

"Now hold on Gee. Just hear me out."

"How the hell do you know my real name? Who the fuck are you? What do you want?" I drag my jeans roughly over my tender skin, yanking them up and fastening them while I shout at him. I reach for my vests, ignoring my underwear, and pull them over my head when he responds. He stutters out something that I miss because the fabric damn near tears my ears off.

"What was that?"

"You don't even recognise me do you?" He mocks but can't disguise his disappointment.

"You're familiar. I obviously know you from somewhere but right now I'm only concerned with how you fucking know me. My own God-fearing mother wouldn't recognise me if I walked up and smacked her across the face with my birth certificate."

"You might have lost some weight and dyed your hair, Gee but I would recognise you anywhere. I'm a little hurt you can't say the same."

"I never knew anyone named Xadian."

"Sure, and Gigi Shade is your real name I take it?"

So Xadian was a stage name? I guess it had to be. But who was he? There was only one guy who paid me any attention back then: Dean Kincaid. He was the one person I had crushed on like a loser—the one guy as screwed up as me—but even he didn't think I

34

was good enough for him. I seriously doubted he would make such an effort to find me. He would have forgotten me the moment I skipped town. It couldn't be Dean. Yeah, the almond shaped eyes were his and that thick lower lip, that could be his. *Shit!*

"The last thing I said to you was "Look in the mirror, Regina. See what I see when I look at you," he whispers, his mouth pulls tight. He is pained.

"Dean?" Xade nods.

"I told you to ask yourself if that was enough for you. If you were happy to be what everyone else expected you to be for the rest of your life. The next day you were gone," he adds confirming that he is that same boy.

I ache hearing him repeat those words. They were the last straw for me. I had rummaged up the courage to confront him that day. We were at school, in the parking lot just before my mother showed up in, what the other kids called, her 'Jesus wagon'. I dragged my feet over to the low wall where he always sat with his friends and called out his name with a trembling voice.

"What the hell do you want God-Girl?" One of his crew sneered but he ignored it and followed me a few feet away.

"I know, I know you hate me," I began, "and I'm not sure what I have done to deserve that, but I would really like it if you could lay off me. Things are really difficult and I...Why Dean? Why don't you like me?" I stumbled. The verbal diarrhea embarrassed us both. We were as red-faced as each other. I remember a split second where his glare softened before he put his great verbal boot in my gut.

"Wake the fuck up, Regina! You need to deal with the fact that I don't want you, God-Girl." He raised his voice and turned slightly to make sure his friends were watching. They were. "I know how your pretty white panties get wet every time you look at me, but honestly, Regina, dipping my cock in you would be like splashing it around in the church font. Perhaps you should follow in your mother's footsteps and dedicate yourself to God? At least you know *he* wants you." I heard the others laughing, hissing and jeering behind him. He heard it too. He lowered his voice and his cold eyes softened again.

"Look in the mirror, Regina. See what I see when I look at you. Ask yourself if that is enough. Are you so happy to be who everyone else expects you to be? Can you carry on like this forever? Really look, Regina, and maybe you will see that this isn't who you really are." He turned on his thick biker-boot heel and stormed back to the crowd. I saw him glance at me and shake his head one last time before my life imploded. I was gone by the next morning and until now, I hadn't looked back.

"Fuck! *Fuckfuckfuck!*"

"I take it that it wasn't enough?"

"Stuck in a dead end town? Living a dead end life? No fucking way! I was nobody and nothing there and you, Dean, you made me feel like less than nothing!" He frowns at the reminder. I do too because I hadn't meant to sound so hurt when I said it.

36

"Screw that. It is done. Over with. I'm a different person now. Look, Xade, Dean, whatever you call yourself now. I don't understand why you are here, or more pertinently, why you sought me out for a sweet little fuck, but now that it's done I really would like you to fuck-the-hell-off and forget you know me. If you dare to tell anyone about who I was or where I came from, I promise you I will have someone hunt you down, rip your cock off and shove it up your ass. Now, if you don't mind, I have to phone Snowflake and tell him he got the director's job."

"You're firing me?"

"Were you really here for the job?"

"I… No."

"Didn't think so."

"Gee, baby, wait. I meant what I said before. I made a promise. I handled this all wrong, I know that. I mean, I never intended to fuck you today—"

"Really. That is a shame. That was the best part of our reunion."

"Fuck it woman! Will you just hear me out? I am not the dick I was back then. I wasn't even really being that big of a dick. Well I was, but it was for all the right reasons. I just did it in the wrong way. Shit I am not making this any better. Just let me explain properly. Please."

"I don't need to hear it. Like I said, it is a long time gone. Water under the bridge. *Blah blah blah.*"

"Gee!" he shouts in exasperation.

"Get out!" I scream back. I do not want to know. I do not need his pity or his apology or whatever karma-placating action he is making here. I simply want him gone so I can stop feeling like I have just been victim to another of his humiliations. Would he go home and tell everyone that he screwed little Regina—little God-Girl—the town joke? Would they laugh with him and crow about how far the mighty had fallen? Well fuck them.

"What the fuck is going on in here?"

Jenny's screeching voice rebounds around the room. We both turn to face her with wide-eyed guilty expressions. From our mutual undressed state, I can imagine what her reaction will be. Jenny, however, manages to surprise me and instead of railing at me for ruining another video before it got started, she jumps to my defence.

"What the hell did you do to her?" she yells at Xade. I try to calm her down but she positions herself between us like a body shield.

"Jen, it is okay. We messed around but that's not a big deal."

"Not a big deal? You are fucking crying, Gee. You never cry. So this motherfucker is either a dead man walking or he can perform miracles, and Gee, he doesn't look like the son of God to me."

My fingers trace my eyes and—*holy shit*—I am crying.

"I'm sorry Gee," Xade whispers. "I didn't mean to stir things up. I just wanted to see you again. I've thought of nothing else since the day you didn't show up for school."

"Please," I beg not bothering to hide the tears now. It's all too late for that. "Please, just stop. I need you to go."

38

"You heard her!"

"Okay, I will go but use the footage. It will be good. You saw my vision. You liked the concept. Let me give you that. Consider it an apology." He was begging. He leans forward reaching out for me, but Jen slaps his hand away.

"Okay," I manage to reply. I watch him turn on his heel and grab for the door. The action is a startling echo of the last time we parted. This time I feel even more distraught. The first time he left me broken, this time I am shattered. Before he exits, he leaves me with one last promise.

"I always keep my word, Gee."

His exit takes with him the last of my strength and I collapse to the floor. I can feel the years of being Gigi draining from me. She is like makeup that I never wash off. I just reapply a little more of her every day to pretend that I'm not the silly, lonely girl I once was. Yet here, in a pile of flesh and sweat upon the floor, I realise that I am still her. I always was her and I always would be.

"Gee?" Jen bumbles around beside me picking up my discarded underwear and handing it to me timidly.

"It is okay, Jen. I will be okay."

"Want me to cheer you up, Angelface?" she asks, stroking my cheek.

"Sure. What have you got for me?"

"Lusferatu are in town. I just spoke to Sam and she says that the band is using her place for rehearsals before their set this coming weekend. If we can get to them before they play in the bar, we might be able to sign them before Forrester and the other big labels can get to them."

"That's great news." It was. I just wished I could feel more enthusiastic about it, if only for Jen's sake.

"The film crews will be here in under an hour. What do we want to do?" she asks. I hate her practicality but we have too much riding on this to fuck it up. I need to get a hold of myself. I think about work for a minute and then click back into Gigi mode.

"Fire them. Keep the post-production people. We will not need any serious kit for what I have in mind. With any luck we will have the video by the end of the week."

"You sure?"

"Yeah, Xadian might not be the right person for the job, but he had some good ideas. We will use the footage he got today and work from there." Jen nods hesitantly. She doesn't believe me, but I don't care. I have had enough for today. I would focus on signing the new band and get this business moving in the right direction. No matter what feelings Dean's, Xadian's, appearance dragged up, one thing was certain: I was going to make my life worthwhile. I would make sure that every decision I'd made up to now counted for something. As for Xadian, he could shove his promises. If I never saw him again it would be too soon. Although, if that was true why did I hurt more for thinking it? Why did I miss the feel of his body pressed against mine and why was I praying that he was truly a man of his word?

"Gee, maybe we should just postpone the meeting? You can rest and make up your mind later."

I forced a smile to my face, forced Gigi to the forefront once again, forced Regina back into her hiding place, deep within me, and said something that I trusted sounded comforting. "Don't worry yourself, Jen. These things have a way of working themselves out."

I could only pray it was true because I doubted I could survive Xadian for a third time and there was no doubt in my mind that we would meet again. If my time living with my devoutly religious mother taught me anything it was that God had a mean sense of humour and I was ever the butt of the joke.

THE WHITE WOLF

By Kathryn M. Hearst

Once upon a time there were three princesses. All who beheld them said that they were beautiful. The king, who knew their temperaments well, understood that what is pleasing on the outside is not always pleasing on the inside. Though he loved each of the princesses, it was the youngest that he secretly cherished most of all.

On his way back to the castle from a visit to a distant land, the king chose gifts for his three daughters. For the eldest and most spoiled, he chose a necklace made of sapphires to match her deep blue eyes. For the middle princess and the cruelest, he commissioned a gown to be made of the finest golden thread, to match her glowing blonde hair. For his precious Ruby, the youngest, he sent a maid to the forest to collect only white flowers and weave them into a wreath for her hair.

The king waited impatiently by the side of the road for the maid to return, but hours passed and still the maid did not emerge from the forest. The king's heart was heavy as the sun set in the distant sky. He climbed into his carriage and resumed his journey home, without a gift for the youngest princess.

While he was just a few miles from the castle, he saw a large white wolf sitting along the side of the road. Upon his head was a wreath of the most beautiful white flowers the king had ever seen. He called to his coachman to climb down and retrieve the wreath from the wolf.

When the wolf heard the order he laughed deep in his belly and said, "My Lord, I will gladly give you my wreath of the purest white, but I must have something in return."

"Name your price," said the king. "I will give you treasures in exchange for it. It is a gift for my precious daughter, Princess Ruby. Only the purest of flowers may grace her sweet head."

"I don't want treasure, only your promise to give me the first thing that meets you on your way to the castle," the wolf replied with a smile of the purest white teeth.

The king nodded. "I am miles from home, we are certain to meet a wild animal or a bird on the road. I promise. The first thing that meets me will be yours."

The wolf nodded and padded his way to the carriage, where he dipped his head and allowed the king to pull the wreath from his head. The king was so enchanted with the flowers that he failed to notice when the carriage rolled past the palace gates with the white wolf strolling alongside.

"My Lord, Father!" called the youngest princess. It was her tradition to meet her father at the gates each time he returned home. Precious Ruby's eyes were bright as he stepped from the carriage with the wreath of white, but when she saw the sadness in his eyes she grew frightened.

"Dearest Ruby, you must go with the white wolf, for I was tricked into a promise and as a man and a king, I must honor my promises." The king wept bitterly as he placed the wreath upon her head.

The princess hugged her father, his tears breaking her heart into tiny, sharp fragments. "I understand, Father. Please don't weep for we will see each other again."

The white wolf gently closed his mouth over her arm and swung the princess onto his back and took her into the forest. To his delight and surprise, she did not weep and wail. Instead the princess looked at the passing forest in silent wonder.

"Why do you stare at the forest?" the wolf asked.

"I have never been outside of the palace gates."

"Hold tight, precious Ruby, and I will show you things you have never dreamt of." The wolf threw his head back and howled as she curled her fingers into his fur. He ran, and ran, until they came to a stately manor house surrounded by thick forest.

"This is your home?" the princess asked as he knelt to allow her to dismount.

"It is our home," the wolf replied.

***

The whisper of silk on bare flesh followed each step as the princess wove her way through the forest, a skip here and there, her steps were light and carefree. Midnight hued hair hung about her shoulders to the middle of her back. Curious, pale blue eyes searched for new discoveries and her rosy lips curled into smile.

The afternoon sun peeped through the green canopy of leaves, warming the path to the river. In the distance she saw the sunlight dancing upon the water, like a tumble of jewels on silk. She ran toward the water until her slippered feet were forced to tread lightly between fallen logs and rocks.

The sounds of water grew louder as she approached the waterfall and its forbidden cave—the one place the white wolf forbad her to visit. After nearly a year with him, it was also only remaining area of the forest and manor house that she had not thoroughly explored. Drawing up her courage, she set her feet upon the stony path to the grotto. The mist rolled out around her as she neared the falling water. Almost there… a few more feet to travel and she would be in the cave behind the falling water.

A creature growled a warning as she stepped into the misty darkness. Ruby's voice was thin as gossamer. "Who is there?"

A deep, slow voice rumbled in the stone beneath her feet, it hissed in her ears and vibrated through her heart. Something was moving toward her. She felt it nearer, only to startle at the voice so near her ear—a familiar voice. So close that his hot breath caressed her cheek. "I am here… precious Ruby. Why are you in the one place that I forbade in all of the forest? Do you know what happens to princesses who disobey?"

A chill ran through her as the white wolf inhaled her scent and exhaled his moist, warm breath along her arm. "Please, I did not mean to disturb you. I should not have come here."

The wolf moved behind her, blocking her escape. "But you did… go ahead, step further in."

The cave was dark as a moonless night. In the year she spent with the white wolf, she had never once been frightened. Though now, in this dark place she struggled to keep her breathes from coming too fast.

"I have missed the presence of a human female." The wolf's voice sounded different in the cave, less animal, yet more sinister somehow.

"I should go…I will instruct the servants to prepare a lovely dinner for you tonight. I will read to you by the fire, you enjoy it so." She turned with her arms before her to find him in the darkness.

She stopped moving as something hard and sharp pressed against her chest. It had to be his claw, though she dared not reach for him to be sure. "Why do you sound different? Are you ill?"

"I am hungry." The sharp point slid down the front of her blouse, opening the silk from neck to naval.

Ruby's voice trembled as she whispered, "Please, let me go see to dinner. I am a better companion than meal."

He traced along the satin with that felt more like a human finger than the sharp edge of a claw. "I am not hungry for food, my love."

Ruby reached forward to run her fingers through his thick fur, as she had done so many times before. The wolf hissed and moved away, leaving her searching the space between them. "I want to see you."

"You have seen me many times."

Ruby tilted her head to the side, he sounded distracted. A cool draft made her aware that her breasts were exposed. She gasped and pulled the fabric closed, surprised by the sharp intake of air from the white wolf. "Please, you are frightening me."

"You need not be frightened of me, precious Ruby. We have been together for almost a year. In all that time have I ever hurt you?" he whispered from beside her.

Ruby raised her hand at her side, flexing her fingers until they brushed against him. "Where is your fur?"

"Here, in this cave, I am a man." He pressed his hand to her belly, then slowly drew his fingers up her flesh until they grazed her breast.

"Will you let me see you? How do I know you are the white wolf, my wolf?" She batted his hand from her chest.

He grabbed her slender arm and turned her abruptly to face him. "Do you know my voice?"

"I do," Ruby whispered.

"You would not know this face, if I shared it." He brushed his lips across hers, lingering but for one moment, before they moved to her neck.

"Your touch is soft." Ruby resisted the urge to raise her hands to his face, to see him with her fingers, if not with her eyes.

"Only because I don't want to frighten you... I would prefer something much different."

Ruby's eyes grew wide, though his words thrilled her to her core. "You still have not told me what my punishment will be."

"So now you wish to discuss punishment?" His laughter filled the cave with the same deep rumble as his growl had moments before. "Come."

He took her hand as she gathered her shirt closed and hurried along after him. They wound deeper into the dark cave, until a soft glow began to light their way. Ruby dared a look at him but could only make out a strong jaw and light colored hair. He came to a stop at a rock jutting out from the wall, surrounded on either side by small natural pools. Steam rose from the calm surface, rippled each time a droplet of water fell from the stalactites above.

He looked her over slowly as she spoke in a quiet rumble. "Remove your blouse."

Ruby's cheeks turned a soft shade of pink as she slid the ruined silk from her shoulders. She dipped her chin and crossed her arms across her chest to protect her modesty.

"I promised you adventure on our first day together... Do you regret leaving your family and coming with me?" He watched her thoughtfully.

Ruby shook her head. "No. I miss my family, but I love my life here."

He stepped forward and cupped her face with his hand, and lifted her chin until she met his gaze. Ruby stared into the stranger's face with wide eyes. There was something hauntingly familiar in the human face. The eyes, the eyes belonged to the white wolf. He released her face and reached behind her and pulled the tie at the top of her simple wrap skirt. The thin fabric fell lightly at her feet.

"You asked of punishment?" His lips curled into a wolfish grin. "It will be quite pleasurable."

"For you or for me?" Ruby laughed lightly to hide her uncertainty. Her heart hammered in her chest, but for the first time she felt a dull ache between her thighs. Butterflies filled her stomach and threatened to buckle her knees.

"We shall see." He reached out suddenly and pressed her back against the cold wet rock. She gasped and sucked in air, which permitted him to pin her ever harder. "Reach up and put your hands in the bindings."

Ruby began to tremble in earnest. Her thin panties provided no protection at all from the rock or the chilled water on its surface. Fear replaced her earlier feelings of excitement. "I won't run. Please, don't chain me."

"Reach up." He pushed on her stomach, forcing air from her and prompting her to stretch her hands up. Her hands slipped easily through the cuffs, so she reached higher and wrapped her fingers around the cold chains above the bindings.

The man's fingers slowly and carefully dragged down the front of her chest, leaving her shivering. The chill brought goose bumps to her skin and hardened her nipples. Ruby met his hungry gaze and wondered, for the first time, if she would ever walk out of this cave.

"Do you still wish to see me as a wolf?" he asked curiously.

Ruby nodded. "Yes. I love the white wolf, he would never hurt me. If you are truly him, then show me."

In the blink of an eye, the man was gone and the huge white wolf sat before her among the pile of his ruined clothes. Ruby exhaled a relieved breath. A growl rose from deep within the wolf, guttural, and thick enough to touch as it grew louder and traveled up through his body. He seemed to hold his breath a moment, then breathed out through his muzzle sending a hot blast of moist air upon her rounded breasts. She rattled the shackles as she turned her head and jerked away from the wolf. The idea that he would take her in wolf form forced a cry from her.

"Do you still prefer me as a wolf, my precious Ruby?" His voice thinned with humor that ended in a chuckle.

Ruby shook her head quickly.

"Close your eyes," the white wolf said, still grinning.

She closed her eyes tightly, a moment later she felt human hands brush her face as he tied a piece of cloth over her eyes. She dared not speak, or ask why he blindfolded her. Instead she wrapped her fingers tighter around the chains and waited.

Ruby heard a snap from overhead and a moment later she felt his warm breath at her neck. His lips moved slowly across her flesh, then he drew her skin between his teeth and sucked gently. He pulled back and her skin cooled instantly. He pressed something cold and wet against her lips. It took her a moment to remember the icicles hanging from the tips of the stalactites. Her lips parted and he slid the ice into her mouth.

The ice was replaced with his mouth, this time he kissed her hard, crushing her lips as his tongue invaded her mouth. Ruby had seen men and women kiss at court in her father's castle, but never had she seen a kiss like this. He devoured her mouth, making things low in her belly clench and ache.

His hand grasped her waist, while he traced a cold wet line across her bare neck and down to her breast. Her nipple instantly hardened beneath the ice, only to be warmed by his skillful tongue a moment later. She couldn't catch her breath, each movement shocking her system with the quick change from icy chill to burning heat.

Now she understood why he hadn't locked the shackles. She was grateful for them, as her hands gripped the chains until her knuckles were white. They were all that kept her standing.

The icy taper continued downward, pausing at her navel and painting a chilled circle. He breathed lightly upon it, further melting the ice, although her mounting body heat was thawing the thin scales of ice rather quickly. He ran his tongue around her belly button, then dragged his teeth over the curve of her hip bone.

Ruby turned her head to the side and buried her face in her arm, certain she would offend him if she cried out. Even though his breath was warm, the palm of his hand against her waist was comparatively hot. She felt him rise again and the brush of his hair against her cheek as his tongue roamed over her neck and traced her ear.

She felt his warm breath as she whispered impossibly low, "Ruby... your heartbeat has quickened, I hear it pounding in your chest and see the rise and fall of your breasts with each breath." The last words mumbled as he kissed her neck again. She shivered then realized the melting ice taper was slipping between her thighs.

She braced herself for what she thought was next, but it only served to tighten her, making the entry of the ice a greater shock against the heat he had fueled within her. He didn't pause, sliding the ice inside her opening until she cried out, rattling the shackles in the moment of frozen pain as he broke the thin membrane of her maidenhood.

Ruby squirmed as he began to work the ice in slow strokes, in and out of her body. She no longer cared about offending him, begging for it to stop. She twisted against the cuffs to free herself, but his hand held fast to her and his chest kept her pinned against the rock wall. She could barely hear his words for her mind was overcome with the extreme cold that began between her thighs and extended seemingly to her core.

"Shh... I will warm you soon enough, but first you will warm me."

Her voice was slow to rise from her throat. "How, anything, please, stop." It was so difficult to think or form words with the ice melting between her thighs. Surely her warmth would melt it quickly, though not quickly enough.

He chuckled as he traced a path of kisses down her neck and between her breasts. He bit each nipple roughly suckling, as he gently raked a fingernail down the outline of her body sending chills down her spine.

"How... how shall I warm you?" her voice trembled.

His voice hissed in her ear again, "So eager to please... after nothing more than this?" His tongue lashed warmth beneath her ear as she felt the icicle slip from her body and his warmth move away, leaving her exposed.

Ruby's trembling had changed to shaking, her entire body shivered from both the chill in the air and anticipation. She tried to answer, but her teeth chattered fiercely.

"You're cold. Perhaps I should warm you first?"

She still could see nothing of him, yet she felt him shifting closer to her to her thighs. His hot breath trailed across her sex, making her jerk her hips back against the wall. His hands slid along her hips, to her inner thighs, easily parting her legs. His soft hair brushed across her naval, making her jerk again. His grip tightened, holding her in place.

His hot tongue snaked between her thighs as he held her in place. She held her breath and bit her lower lip to keep from speaking. This was... this was so wrong... people didn't kiss each other like this, not there. His tongue lashed up through her soft folds and the warm smooth texture met her nub. Leaving her gasping and clinging to the chains.

She could barely hold on when his tongue began to work in earnest, moving in long, yet quick strokes over her slit, each time rolling over the tiny bundle of nerves. As he continued, he buried his face between her thighs and pulled her body forward. His warm labored breathing rolled over her skin while the heat of his agile tongue explored deeper inside. Her breasts heaved and stomach flexed as his work between her legs pushed her further into an abyss of pleasure. All decorum forgotten, she moaned against her arm.

His chuckle vibrated through her, his face still pressed between her thighs. He extracted his tongue abruptly, leaving an ache between her legs that stole her breath. It took a moment before she realized that he was undoing her blindfold. When she opened her eyes, he was looking at her with an amused expression.

"It is time for you to warm me."

"Now? Is there no more? I ache with need." She looked at him, naked and uninhibited in his arousal. Her eyes widened a fraction before she turned her gaze to the wall beside her.

"Oh, so you want more?" He chuckled.

Ruby blushed deeply, embarrassed to think of what he must think of her. She lowered her lashes and dipped her chin. He stepped before her and cupped her face in his hand, then leaned in and claimed her mouth.

"You must never be ashamed of your desires." He glanced around the cave and sighed. "I would make you warm all night, if I had a soft place to lay you down."

"What about the soft grass near the river?" Ruby offered with a soft smile.

"I will become a wolf the moment I step out of this cave." He frowned and looked at her, as if seeing her for the first time. He reached up and eased her hands from the cuffs, rubbing her wrists gently.

"Where do you sit or rest while you are here?" Ruby glanced about the dimly lit cave.

"I sit on the rocks or bathe in the pools. I do not sleep here. I sleep in the manor house, in a bed, beside you." He grinned as he watched her contemplate.

"Perhaps we could stand, as before?"

"So determined to find a place to make love? You must have enjoyed my tongue." His low voice vibrated through the cave and radiated through her body.

He retrieved the remnants of his clothing and spread them on a relatively flat rock, then lifted her and set her on the edge and knelt before her. Ruby drew her lower lip between her teeth, unsure if she should lie back. He parted her knees and moved between her thighs, then rested his palm on her chest and pushed gently as he dipped his head lower. She leaned back on her elbows, her head falling blissfully back as he sucked her nub between his teeth.

He reignited her heat almost instantly as he alternated between suckling and moving his tongue in quick strokes over the sensitive area. She tensed when she felt his fingers probing her tender folds. "Shhhh, relax." He breathed the word across her as he slid a finger inside her body.

Ruby whimpered and tried to move her hips, to get him to the right place, the place that felt the best, but his fingers tightened on her hip, more or less holding her in place. Soon, she was unable to control her quivering thighs or the jerky motions of her hips—it was too much, the pleasure continued to build until she was certain she could take it no more. Suddenly her body went rigid and then exploded in wave after wave of ecstasy, leaving her writhing and breathless.

He stood and lifted her body, turning her quickly so that he was seated on the ledge and she was in his lap, facing him. He reached down his body and angled himself toward her and pushed his hard flesh into her body without a word. Before she could puzzle out the sudden change in position, or recover from her first orgasm, they were joined.

Ruby cried out, partially in pain, but mostly in pleasure. He did not move for a long moment. His breath had gotten shallow, his face tense. Unsure of what to do, Ruby moved her hips forward slightly her fingers dug into his shoulders. He moved deeper within her then withdrew and pressed in again, a bit further. Gradually, with this halting movement, he worked his way in, helped her accept him, at least as much of his length as her depth would allow.

When he was pressed hard at her core, he paused again. "Ruby?" His voiced trembled through them both, as she held a long breath.

She released the breath in a hoarse, "Yes."

It was enough and all she could say to confirm that having him fill her was bearable. He spread his legs wider grasped her hips in his hands, easing her up and down his shaft in slow strokes, always careful not to exceed his previous depth.

Ruby was panting. Her hands barely clasped behind his neck as he held her. She shifted with his motion inside her. Her long hair had fallen forward, covering her breasts as his strokes quickened, pushing her limits. She pressed her mouth to his shoulder and was surprised when he cried out, her teeth digging into his flesh as his thrusts tore another orgasm from her body.

Her muscles gripped him over and over again as she moaned against his shoulder. She felt him tense, then the rush of his seed filled her. His deep moans became a low roar. Slowly, as they came back to themselves, he drew her closer still and held her in his arms. Her panting moans were now nearly whimpers. She shook within his embrace, shivering with the last shock waves of her own pleasure, however stressful it may have been on her body.

When he had mind to speak and energy to move, the smooth curve of a fingernail brushed her cheek, pushing back a lock of midnight hued hair from her face. His breath was warm again, though his voice was still hushed. "I've wanted to do this with you many times since I brought you to my home."

Ruby smiled shyly, though her eyes remained closed. "May we do it many times more?"

"Yes, but not here." He kissed the top of her head. "It is time that I break this curse."

Ruby hadn't had time to wonder about the cave or the magic that allowed him to be a man inside the dark place. "How can it be broken?"

"If I tell anyone how to break the curse, it will become permanent."

"Then how will I know what to do to break it?" She tilted her head, puzzling over the situation in her mind. Would it be telling if he gave her riddles to solve? She looked back to him, her brows knitted together. "I do not know your name."

He shook his head slowly. "I cannot remember my name."

He stood and set her to her feet. "You must go back to your family. It has been a year, and your eldest sister is to be married. We will leave tonight."

"Leave you?" Ruby was perplexed.

"You said tonight, you missed your family." He replied as he began to guide her from the cave.

"I do, but I don't want to leave you." She smelled the mist before she heard the roar of the falls. Her heart pounded in her chest as she grew closer to the exit of the cave.

"I will see you to the palace gates, and will after the wedding to bring you home." He stepped past her, onto the slippery rocks beneath the waterfalls. The moment his body passed the invisible barrier of the cave, he became the white wolf.

Ruby climbed onto his back with a heavy heart. She was so troubled that she failed to realize that she was naked on his back. He took her to the manor house and waited while she went to her room. Lying on her bed was the most beautiful gown. It looked to be made of starlight, spun into cloth. Beside the gown was a necklace of the most unusual stones. They looked like sunlight was trapped within them. When she walked out the front door of his home her steps were slow and heavy, despite the lovely gifts.

"I don't want to go," she said quietly. When he didn't reply, she climbed onto his back and wrapped her arms around his neck, burying her face in his fur.

White wolf ran through the forest as night began to settle. He ran and ran, until he came to the road near the palace gates. "My precious Ruby, take the wreath of flowers from my head and remember me. I will come here after the wedding. Come when you hear me howl. You must come when I call or you will never find your way back to me in the forest."

Ruby was so distraught that she hadn't noticed the wreath of flowers on the beloved wolf's head. She removed the flowers and placed them on her head. "What shall you remember me by?"

"Perhaps a kiss, my love?" He knelt down and she placed a tearful kiss on his muzzle.

Behind her horns began to blow and someone shouted her name from the great wall, surrounding the palace. She turned to see several guards coming through the gates and when she turned back the white wolf was gone.

Ruby was taken to her parents, the king and queen. Though she was happy to see them, her heart was broken.

"My precious Ruby, where is your pure heart and constant smile?" her father asked from the dais.

"I left them in the forest with the white wolf." Ruby sighed.

"Nonsense. You are simply tired from your ordeal. Go to your room and rest before the ceremony."

Hearing the news of their youngest sister's return, the women came to her room to see the girl for themselves. Since she had been gone, their father had made it clear to them and all of the kingdom that Ruby was his greatest joy and a hero for bearing the weight of his foolishness with grace and dignity. How they hated their sister when she was born, but they hated her ten-fold after she was taken into the forest.

"Dear sister, how happy I am to see you again. What a lovely necklace. I will have it as a wedding gift." The eldest sister stepped forward and snatched the jewels from her slender neck.

"Of course, you should have the necklace. It matches your golden hair," Ruby said solemnly.

"What gift did you bring for me, little sister?" The middle sister looked down her nose at Ruby, seeing her hands were empty and no more jewels.

"You may have my wreath of the purest white flowers. A gift from my love, the white wolf." Ruby whispered.

"I don't want your flowers. I want the dress, it will look better on me anyway. Besides, why do you need such a dress living in the forest with the animals?" her sisters cackled and laughed.

"Oh no, I don't live with the animals. I live in a beautiful manor, with servants, and lovely rooms. I am free to do as I wish, to explore and learn as I wish. The white wolf is a prince." Ruby gushed on and on, the more she spoke of the white wolf the higher

her heart flew. It flew so high that she failed to see the jealous expressions on her sister's faces.

"Well. We must go and prepare for the wedding," the middle sister said. "Take off my dress. I will not have you wear it at court."

The eldest linked her arm with the middle sister and laughed as they left Ruby alone.

Ruby dressed for the wedding in plain blue dress she had worn many years before. A part of her felt sorry for her sisters. Since she was born, she had been the king's favorite—it had to be difficult for them. Now, she had found her true love and was free of the rules and duty of living at court. She had a lovely home and a handsome prince. While her eldest was to marry a Duke, and the middle sister was yet to be betrothed. Perhaps she would invite them to the forest for a vacation one day soon.

The ceremony was long, and boring, though the chapel was decorated in all manner and color of flowers, all except white. Ruby thought of the white wolf's wreath sitting on her bed and smiled. It wouldn't be long now and she would hear his howl and return to her home in the forest, or the cave to make love again.

The wedding feast was as extravagant as the ceremony, though not as dull. Midway through the celebration, the king had ordered the musicians to play in honor of the bride and groom, and her return. She danced and danced, until her feet felt too small for her slippers. Her mother and father were over the moon to see her and she was surrounded by their love as the hour grew late. Still, she hadn't forgotten the white wolf, and listened for his call.

Once, she thought she heard the call, but it was short and could not be her love calling her home. The cry of a wolf was long and mournful, no, the yelp she heard had to be that of a dog. The bride and groom retired, and still the party continued. Ruby began to grow weary. Why had he not come? Perhaps he was being generous, allowing her so much time with her family.

"My Lord, Father, have you seen my sister?" Ruby asked as her father pulled her to the dance floor once again.

"She is wed and with her husband." He laughed and spun her around the floor, as he had done when she was a child.

"The other sister, Father." Ruby giggled.

"No, my precious one." Ruby smiled when her mother came to claim her husband for a dance. She was thankful to have one last dance, but it was time for her to go to the gates. Certainly, the white wolf was waiting for her by now.

Ruby made her way to the gates and looked out to the side of the road where he promised to meet her, but he wasn't there. She paced in front of the gate for some time and still he did not come.

"Why do you pace in front of the gates? There is a wedding and a party for the returned princess inside." A young guard called to her from the wall.

Ruby thought to tell him that she was the princess, but decided to be cautious. What if her father ordered them to keep her inside? "I was hoping to see the white wolf. Someone told me he would be here to collect the princess."

"Oh, you are too late. He came and took the girl in the dress of spun starlight into the forest... hours ago."

Ruby couldn't believe what she had heard. How could her sister run off with the white wolf? Worse, how could he mistake her for her sister? If he loved her, as he promised he did, wouldn't he notice the difference? "Please, can you open the gates? If I have missed the white wolf, then it is passed time for me to return home."

***

Ruby wandered the forest for days and days, and still she could not find her way back to the white wolf's manor. Her dress was tattered and torn and her hair had grown white from grief. She slept in hollowed logs and ate berries to keep up her energy for the search. Berries alone were not enough sustenance for a young woman and soon she became as frail as a dandelion.

One clear day, when no wind blew through the trees, Ruby came upon a small cabin. Smoke rose from the chimney, so she thought someone was home. She knocked lightly on the door.

"Come in," a voice from within answered.

Ruby pushed open the weathered door and was surprised to see nothing but a swirling wind in the middle of the room. "Hello?"

"Yes, old woman. I am right here." Laughed the wind as it surrounded her, blowing her hair from her face. "Oh forgive me, young lady. I thought you were... never mind. What may I do for you?"

"I am searching for the white wolf. Have you seen him?" Ruby asked.

"I have blown for days and nights, to and from, and I have not seen the white wolf," he answered. "Here, take the shoes by the door. They will allow you to travel two hundred miles with each step. Surely, you will find him with them."

Ruby put on the shoes and went outside, a curious thing happening as she took a step. Each step she took was not forward, but up. She walked up and up, until she came upon a star. Perhaps the star knew where the white wolf lived. After all, he had given her a gown of spun starlight.

"Dear star, have you seen the white wolf?" Ruby asked the glowing beauty.

"No, Princess, I have not seen the white wolf. He may stay inside his manor in the evening. Perhaps you should ask the sun?" the star replied and blew Ruby a kiss.

Ruby caught the kiss in the palm of her hand, but the kiss continued to move through space until she found herself face to face with the sun.

"Princess? Where is the necklace of my light? I am surprised you are not wearing it." The sun looked at her from head to toe, but he had the sense not to comment on her haggardly appearance.

"I gave the necklace to my eldest sister as a wedding gift. Please, have you seen the white wolf? I must get home to him."

"I have seen him. He is at his manor in the forest, but you are too late. He is no longer a wolf. His curse was broken by another. They are to marry tomorrow."

"Oh, no." Ruby hid her face in her hands and wept.

The sun, being a father of three girls himself, took pity on the youngest princess. "I will help you."

Ruby's tears turned to bright yellow stones, set inside a crown of gold. "Is it not too late?"

"Perhaps, but perhaps not. I will set you down at the palace of the white wolf. Inside the garden you will find a spinning wheel, it will spin sunlight into thread. Go and work the wheel until your sister comes. You will know what to do from there."

"Thank you," Ruby said, though she did not know what to do from there, or how to find her love.

The sun did as he said and slid Ruby down a beam of sunlight, into the garden of the white wolf. This was not the manor house that she so dearly loved, but a castle set high upon a mountain. Ruby sat down and begun to spin sunlit thread from moss, until her hands were aching and stiff, yet she continued to spin the wheel.

"Old woman, why are you in my garden?" called the middle sister.

"I have brought you gifts." Ruby dared not look into her sister's eyes, for fear she would be recognized. She let her silver-gray hair obscure her face as she worked.

"What gifts can a wretched old woman give me, the future queen?" The middle sister turned to leave, when a sunbeam came forth from the jeweled crown.

"I bring a crown of sunshine for your golden hair and can spin pure sunlight from moss, for your gown." Ruby answered as she spun.

The middle sister snatched the crown from Ruby's feet and lifted her chin so that she stared down her nose. "My wedding is tomorrow. You better hurry."

Ruby sighed in relief as her sister left the garden. Though she had yet to find the white wolf and had no idea of what she would say to him if she found him. With nothing else to do, Ruby spun moss as she tried to think of a plan to win back her love.

"Old woman? Are you well?" The deep masculine voice rang through the garden and straight into Ruby's heart.

"I am working for the princess, my lord. The day is hot and it is lonely work. Would you sit with me for a short while?" Ruby hunched over the wheel, keeping her face hidden behind a veil of tangled hair.

"Of course." He sat on a rock a few feet from the wheel as Ruby continued to work.

"May I tell you a story?" Ruby asked, without looking at him. Her voice raw from thirst, though disguised enough that he didn't recognize her.

"If you wish." He answered softly.

Ruby caught a glimpse of his face and frowned. He looked troubled and heavy hearted, especially for a man who recently had a curse broken and was to be married the next day. She cleared her throat and began. "Once upon a time, a king was tricked into giving his youngest, and most beloved, daughters to a white wolf."

The man sighed. Ruby knew that he knew the story well. Though the townsfolk had twisted him into the villain and the princesses return into a happy ending. She could see that he had no desire to hear the story today of all days, but still she persisted.

"The young princess was not afraid. In fact she grew to love the white wolf. One day, she broke his rules and wandered into a forbidden cave, the only place in all of the forest he asked her not to explore. The princess, you see, had followed the wolf to the cave many times. He would hide in the cave most days and return to her side at night. She missed him dearly." Ruby's voice was even hoarser as her throat tightened and tears fell to her cheeks. She expected him to stop her and sweep her into his arms, but he motioned for her to continue.

"The princess was frightened in the dark cave, but the wolf was there and he promised her adventure. That day, he showed her love and pleasure like no woman has ever known. She never wanted to leave him, or the cave. You see, in the cave the wolf was a man, not a wolf. That very night, the wolf took the princess back to her father's palace for her eldest sister's wedding. The princess didn't want to leave him, but he insisted he would come for her." Ruby paused and murmured, "Shall I continue?"

The man nodded, but did not speak, nor did he look at the old woman.

"When the princess's older sister saw the beautiful gifts the wolf had given her, they took them. No, that is not right. The princess, feeling sorry for her bitter sisters, gave the gifts, all except a wreath made of the purest white flowers. The princess waited and waited, but her wolf never called for her. So she snuck away and wandered the forest for days and days, never finding the white wolf. Her body grew thin, and her hair white in her grief, still she could not find her love. She found the wind, but the wind had not seen the white wolf. She used the wind's shoes to walk to a star, but the star hadn't seen him. The star sent her to the sun… and the sun sent her to the white wolf's palace."

After she grew silent for a long moment, the man stood and looked up at the night sky. She had spun sunlight and her tale well into the evening. "How does the fairy tale end, old woman?"

"I do not know, my Lord." Ruby sighed and continued to spin the wheel as he walked away.

The next day she still sat spinning as the wedding guests began to arrive. By this time she had spun piles and piles of sunlit thread and still she worked—though she didn't know why. The Prince brought the wedding guests into the garden, along with the surprised bride, her sister and parents…still Ruby spun the wheel.

"Answer a riddle, before the wedding." The Prince called to all gathered.

"I lost a key to my treasure chest, so my advisors had a new one made. After some time, I found the old key. Answer me this… which key will open the chest?"

The guests, kings, queens, courtiers, and noblemen all murmured and discussed the riddle. The bride's kingly father answered first, "The old key is better, though you should be careful not to lose it again."

The crowd erupted in laughter, all except Ruby who had stopped spinning and was looking at the prince.

"I see. So then the woman who was first key to my heart, would also be better than the one who was thrust upon me while I searched for the first?" The prince stared at the king for a moment.

"What are you saying?" The middle sister stomped her foot, red faced angry. "What a worthless riddle. I broke the curse, not her."

The prince laughed softly and spread his arms wide, as if waiting for lightening to strike him in the chest. "I would rather live my nights as a wolf and days in a cave, with love... than to live as a man cursed to never love."

As soon as the words left his mouth the sunlit threads that Ruby had spent hour upon hour spinning rose up in a mighty wind. The threads rolled and wove together, forming a cyclone of golden light, with Ruby in the eye of the storm. The sun burst through the clouds and lit the garden, and a single star shone in the midday sky.

When the wind died down, Ruby stood in the center of the garden, in a dress of pure sunlight. On her head was a crown made of diamonds that shown with the light of the stars. Her silvery hair, streaked with midnight hues that brought out her crystal blue eyes, and her rosy lips curled into a lovely smile.

The prince, still a man, had not been struck by lightning—but by love. He knelt before Ruby and with the eyes of the white wolf, asked, "Will you forgive me? I thought you decided not to return. I should have searched for you. I should have never given up."

Ruby took his hand and drew him to his feet. "Will you tell me your name?"

"Rafe. My name is Rafe." He laughed softly as drew her into his arms.

"I forgive you, Rafe." She rose to tip toes and whispered into his ear, "Though there will be many, many nights of punishment."

"Of course." He kissed her lips in the garden, and then once more when they were pronounced husband and wife, and again and again for the remainder of their long days.

THE END

FUCK IT OUT

By Caroline Baker

Early this morning
We got pissed
Over some shit
We both had missed

Had a knock down
Drag out fight
Yelled and screamed
With all our might

Said some things
I knew we'd regret
The kinds of things
That are hard to forget

He stormed out

Said get your shit on track

So I shot two birds

Right at his back

I came home at six

Ready to go

He was in the kitchen

And turned around slow

I could tell by his face

He was feeling the same

Fuck yeah, Baby

Let's start this game

He moved first

Before I could react

He came at me fast

And pushed me back

Till I hit the wall

His hand at my jaw

Held my face still

And I saw

Red as my temper
Flared sky high
Then he used his leg
To part my thighs

He pushed in close
Right in my space
Noted the murderous
Look on my face

And he just smiled
His cocky ass grin
Said listen up, Baby
This shit's gonna end

Now I know you probably
Spent all day
Getting more worked up
Thinking on what you'd say

To me tonight
But I thought all day too
So let me tell you
What we're gonna do

Me and you

Are gonna fuck it out

And we're not stopping

Till there's no doubt

That all the anger

And all the rage

Are fucked away

And we're on the same page

Now you can fight me

And you probably will

But if I'm honest

The thought gives me a thrill

Cause I got some rope

And a brand new paddle

So go ahead, Baby

You've got nothing I can't handle

I tried to respond

But had no chance

His mouth came down hard

As his hand went to my pants

He undid the button
And pulled them down
He bit my lip hard
I gasped and found

His tongue pushing in
Tangling with mine
His hand hit my panties
Aiming to find

My clit and he did
In two seconds flat
Pushed two fingers in
And that was that

Started fucking me hard
And he was relentless
Betrayed by my pussy
And its overwhelming wetness

Fuck but he knew
How to do it just right
And I swear I tried
With all my might

But before I knew it
I was all over his hand
And I swear to Jesus
Here where I stand

He licked every
Finger clean
Said, Fuck you taste good
With a little mean

Mixed with your sweet
And tangy flavor
I'm gonna eat you all night
And I'll totally savor

Every drop, Baby
Gonna wear you out
Till you're all out of things
To be pissed about

He picked me up
So we were face to face
Slapped my ass hard
Said, You want to taste?

And fuck me I did
So I took his mouth again
He headed toward the bedroom
Where he aimed to win

Cause true to his word
My man fucked me right
And drained every ounce
Of my fight

Then we talked for hours
And laughed till we cried
Till we worked it all out
And set it aside

Then he gave me his sweet
And wrapped me up tight
Fuck My Man
Sure knows how to fight

TUG: LOVE AT FIRST SIGHT

By: Bry Dig

Prologue

Shooter slammed his bathroom cabinet. The cabinet rattled and reopened, spilling the contents in to the sink. He cursed in one long never-ending string.

"What the fuck is all this shit? The world is fucking against me. What the fuck?" He spoke between his ground teeth.

Ten minutes later, when Tripp entered the house, Shooter was still painting the air with profanity. When he finally noticed his friend, he glared at Tripp. Pushing past him, Shooter headed for the kitchen.

"You here to tell me not to go?" Shooter demanded as he filled his wallet with a wad of cash he retrieved from a cookie jar.

Tripp leaned against the kitchen doorframe and watched his friend. "Told you what I thought of this. Tour is over, we have two months. Figure I had time to kill. Want company?"

"You know she's mine right? I'm not sharing her. That threesome was a one-time deal." Shooter surveyed his friend trying to decipher what Tripp's true intentions were.

Tripp rolled his eyes. "Yeah your girl has a magical pussy but I am well aware it was a one-time stop."

Shooter bit his lip, the metal ring painfully digging in his teeth. "I'm getting her back."

"She may *not* forgive you dude."

Shooter closed his eyes. He hated the guilt. It filled his body, causing pain to pump around his heart. When he closed his eyes, he replayed the scene over again. Catalina opened the hotel room door. He saw the happiness drain from her. Shooter hadn't had a chance to explain why he did what he did. He didn't have a chance to tell her why his cock was ten full inches deep in another woman. Reaching in his pocket, he fisted the custom made engagement ring that was meant to only be on Catalina's finger.

"I'm just going to have to accept that she may never forgive me but I'm not leaving until she is married to me. That girl is it for me. Love at first sight." Shooter walked past Tripp and picked his bag up from the hallway floor. "I'm headed to the airport now. You coming?"

Tripp nodded his head and followed his friend into the unknown. He smirked, thanking the metal gods it wasn't him falling apart over a girl. "Right behind you man."

Chapter 1

~Isabella~

"Bella open up. Emergency!" Catalina pounded on my door.

Catalina, my best friend, was not one to show up at my home unannounced. We had been friends since just after high school and practically inseparable since then. She never joked around nor called wolf so the *emergency* part of her statement had my heart pounding.

Despite my red booty shorts and my black Death Metal t-shirt, I didn't hesitate to open the door. Catalina looked down at me. Her eyes were watery and rimmed in worry.

"What the hell is going on? Get your ass in here and tell me." Grabbing her wrist, I pulled Catalina into my house, locking the door behind her.

Once the door locked, Catalina spoke frantically. "Shooter Solis was at my door when I got home."

Shooter Solis. I used to be a huge fan of the guy. He was the new drummer to Rising Devils, the hottest metal band on the face of this earth. The guys were sexy and the drums mixed with the guitars made any lame lyric they had sound good. I liked the singer and all, but being a drummer girl myself, I was a huge fan of Shooter. One thing changed my opinion of Shooter Solis. He broke my best friend's heart.

The two of them met at a grocery store and he tracked her down to the strip club where we worked. Being the fan girl I was, I drove him to her apartment. There was a moment when I wasn't going to do it, but something in his eyes told me that he was different. I was wrong. She took off with him for five days and fell in love, only to be heartbroken when he cheated on her. What made it worse was he had proposed to Lina hours before cheating.

I hated the guy now.

"The fucker has some nerve. So what did he say?" I demanded whirling around and facing Lina.

"I ran here without talking to him."

It was like the moon and stars aligned because at that moment someone started pounding on my front door. He must have followed her and Catalina's terrified eyes stilled me. As much as I wanted to tell this jerk to get lost, it wasn't my decision. Whether or not she gave him a second chance was up to her.

"What do you want me to do?" I questioned. She looked at me and then the door.

Softly she spoke, "Gone. I want him gone."

My fire engine red hair swayed from my ponytail as I charged for the door. Yanking it open, I didn't flinch when the door bounced off the wall. I pulled back my arm and punched him dead in his face. Lucky for me, he was leaning against the door frame giving me access to his face. He stumbled back holding his eye. From behind him, Shooter stepped forward.

Fuck! I hit the wrong guy.

"Mother Fucker!" The guy I hit growled out.

Tilting my head I looked at the guy. His hands covered his face but his blue hair fell forward. Looking over my shoulder I spoke to Lina. "Catalinaaaa…." I drew her name out. I was in trouble, I could just feel it. "I might have punched the wrong guy. This one has blue hair."

"Fuck! I think you broke my eye socket you crazy bitch." He bellowed.

Seriously, he was complaining? I hit him hard, sure, but it wasn't hard enough to break something. For heaven's sake my hand wasn't even hurting. The fifty dollars a month I was paying for kick boxing classes didn't seem like a rip off anymore. There would be no more complaining about spending that money. It had done me proud tonight.

"That one is Tripp." Lina pressed her lips together suppressing a smile.

Tripp? I vaguely remembered him. He was also in the Rising Devils band. I think he played the guitar but I thought he had a Mohawk. Either way he was too big to be crying about a punch. "Stop crying like a bitch. If it helps, I thought you were Shooter. Besides, you were pounding on my fucking door so you deserved a punch to the face."

Tripp stood and removed his hands from his face. The guy was tall, real tall compared to my five-two. He returned my glare with one of his own and moved forward, towering over me. Lifting my chin, I stared into his angry face. Damn he was pretty. His silver eyes reflected like mirrors framed in dark lashes. His blue hair was bright but who was I to judge? Mine was bright too. He had a square jaw covered with a shadow of stubble. His dark eyebrows lifted and he gazed down at me. Tripp backed up slightly, looking down at my body. Nothing new for me, I was a stripper and it happened on a regular basis, yet his once over made me squirm. A devilish smile crossed his face. The skin around his eye started to puff and change color. He was too busy eye fucking me to even care. It kind of pissed me off. Here I was trying to defend a friend and there he was fucking me in his head.

"Go ahead and eye fuck me you twat." Flipping Tripp off I turned and faced Lina. "You want to talk to these fools?"

Shooter, who was hanging out behind Tripp, took that moment to move forward. Lina shook her head back and forth and started backing up. I went back in to action mode. Throwing my arm back I readied for another punch but then I was upside down. I didn't even have time to get the punch out Tripp had hauled me up like I was nothing. .My stomach was flung over his broad shoulder with my ass in the air and my face almost plastered against his. Tripp slapped my rear and I cried out, kicking and pounding on his muscular back.

"Let go of me you fuck—" My words cut off when Tripp closed my front door just as Shooter went inside with Lina.

"Listen doll. We didn't catch two different flights, spend two hours trying to rent a car, and sit outside her apartment just for you to stand in our way." Tripp's voice was thick and sounded like he

83

smoked a pack a day. It was sexy as hell. I think he was southern too because like Shooter, he had a drawl.

He put me down and pushed me up against an SUV I assumed was his. With his hips he pinned me against the vehicle. The throbbing in his pants beat against my stomach. Maybe I should have been grossed out but from the outline of his dick I was slightly curious. From what I could feel, he was a big boy. Tripp opened the back door and motioned with his blue head for me to get in. His hair flopped in his face but those grey mirror-like eyes stared at me intensely. I hesitated before climbing in to the back seat.

Tripp climbed in behind me and pulled a pack of cigarettes from his pocket. He offered me one and I declined. I watched him place one in his sexy mouth and light up. The flicker of flame cast an orange glow on his skin and reflected in his silver eyes. His straight nose had a hoop in it and when he tucked his chin length blue hair behind his ear, I caught the sight of the gauges in his earlobes. Along with the tattoos that danced down his arms and decorated his hands, he was everything I normally wasn't attracted to. However on him, all the colorful tattoos and metal adornments gave him that bad boy look that girls like me were suckers for. I would have gone in for a flirty move but I remembered this was Shooter's friend. Shooter who cheated on my best friend.

"He doesn't deserve a second chance you know," I finally found my voice. Crossing my legs, I leaned my head back against the headrest. Shooter had two hundred seconds before I was

84

marching in my house and saving my best friend. I already started counting.

Smoke filled the vehicle. He must have realized he was smoking us out because Tripp flicked his cigarette out the door and closing us back in. "We all deserve a second chance. Like you for example. My first impression of you is that you are a bitch. Don't you want to change that impression?"

"God you are such a guy. No I don't want to change that impression and that's different. A second chance in a relationship where the dude couldn't keep it in his pants is not the same."

"We could be in a relationship you know. You're my style. I saw you checking me out, so I know the feeling is mutual." Tripp laughed and stretched his legs out in front of him as best he could. "Shooter believes in that love at first sight shit. I'm starting to see the logic in it."

I blinked before staring. Was he for real? "Are you joking right now?"

Tripp laughed. His long arms stretched above his head and he laced his fingers together before placing them behind his head. He moved down in his seat and relaxed before closing his eyes. "Naw. Just making convo. We can switch topics though if you want."

"To what?"

"To if I should or shouldn't press charges on you." He opened one eye and a cocky little grin played on his lips. I felt moisture start pooling in my panties. *Son of a bitch got me turned on with a smile.* "I could be convinced not to if you persuaded me. I'm kind of famous so they would totally haul your pretty ass to jail doll. I have a good feeling about that. And if they didn't then I would just sue you."

Sue me? He was joking right? Right?

My mouth fell open. *This was a joke right?* He laughed and dropped his hands holding on to his stomach. He was joking and I felt like a fool for believing him for a second.

"I was just kidding doll. You have a good arm but I don't want it to get out that I got my ass handed to me by a little princess," He winked at me and I rolled my eyes. "A blow job *would* make me feel better though."

"You want me to suck your cock? You're crazy, I don't even know you." My eyes went to his lap. *Was I entertaining this idea? What was wrong with me?* "If anything it would be a hand job."

"Sold!" His response was a little too enthusiastic.

Wait! What happened? I was teasing, wasn't I? My pussy throbbed and my nipples hardened against my shirt. Not wearing a bra made this very obvious.

Tripp must have seen me back-pedaling or something because he slowly moved closer to me. He was testing me out I think, seeing if I would push him away. He tilted his head to the left and leaned in closer. Our breaths mingled. His lips brushed mine then his tongue flicked across my lips. Opening my mouth slightly, he took that moment to slip his tongue between my lips. His tongue pushed at mine and I tasted his cigarette. His hands cupped my face

86

bringing me closer to him. I moved across the seat until I straddled his legs.

There was plenty of space between us, but even with that space I could feel the heat his body radiated. His hands stayed on my face as we kissed but my hands explored. I moved them down his chest feeling him through his shirt. I grazed over the hard lines and dips of his muscles. One nipple was pierced and when I gently pulled at it, he groaned into my mouth. It was a sexy sound, deep and it rumbled in his chest. Wanting more reactions from him, my hands moved down until the tips of my fingers brushed across his cock.

Pulling from his lips, I shoved my hand against his chest and pushed him back. He tried to come back for more kissing but I held him against the seat. Looking down at his shirt, I pulled up the hem and gasped at what I saw. His cock was hard and up his lower abdomen peeking past jeans.

He. Was. Hung.

Hard, he was impressive. Even flaccid, I was positive it would hang half way down his legs. Tensely I reached out and stroked the silken skin of his exposed cock. He was pierced at the head of it, a Prince Albert, but instead of a loop it was a pretty silver barbell. Tripp moved forward again and took my lips with his. His hands fumbled with his jeans and he unbuttoned them, freeing his cock fully. He took my hands in his then placed them on him.

"You want to back out?" Tripp asked me against my lips. His serious tone slapped me in the face. I could back out right now. *But did I want to?*

Wrapping my hand around the base of his cock, I pushed my mouth hard in to his and kissed the fuck out of him. The largest cock I had ever seen, attached to a beautiful man, who was a rock star, made my decision easy. I was going to be the slut tonight. My tongue battled his and my hand moved up his length in one fluid motion. He placed his hands on my waist. My thumb ran over the head of his cock and down across his piercing. Tripp gripped my waist firmly, jerking his hips up, and thrusting his dick through my hands. My fingers flicked over the piercing of his cock, while I was coaxed his tongue with mine. Pre-cum wet my thumb and I spread it across the head of his cock.

Tripp pulled on my bottom lip sucking it between his teeth before he let go. I moved my hand down his cock gripping his length hard. The silky shaft throbbed in my hands and thickened slightly in my grip. My pussy was wet and begging me for this dick. I wasn't sure how long this hand job was going to last because I was ready to ride his pretty cock until I orgasmed.

Tripp moved his mouth to my neck distracting my thoughts. Throwing my head back, I gave him all the access. He licked and kissed. Gripping him with only one hand I used the other to cup his balls. I moved my fingers gently fondling them and Tripp bit lightly at my neck. With a tight grip I tugged up his long shaft reaching the head of his cock again. He bucked his hips thrusting his dick in my hand. My thumb ran over his piercing, toying once more. Tripp held on to my waist tight and threw his head back, abandoning the kisses he was placing on my neck. He squeezed his eyes closed and a second later he came in my hand.

"Three tugs?" I laughed out looking at my hand covered in his cum.

This had never happened to me. Not that I went around giving hand jobs, but most lasted a little longer. Laughter bubbled in me and I snorted as I laughed harder.

He panted and looked up at me with intense eyes. "It was your grip."

Wiping the cum on my hand, onto his shirt, I laughed and bailed out of the SUV. His hands tried to stop me but I escaped. My stomach tightened as I laughed. Three tugs! Wow, good thing I didn't have sex with the guy. It would have been over before it started. Laughing again I barged in to my own home. Looking behind me Tripp was close behind, shirtless and suspiciously pulling up his jeans. Turning back to my house I smiled wide at Catalina. She smiled back with a questionable look. I flipped Shooter off as I passed him then headed straight for my friend.

"This fool wanted me to make up for the punch by sucking his cock." I laughed and doubled over before standing back up. "So we compromised…" God I couldn't stop laughing. My words were barely audible. They were reaching high-pitched tones only dogs and dolphins could understand. Tripp stood next to Shooter with his arms crossed. His eyes looked… amused. "…hand job…three tugs and he blew."

Catalina cracked a smile then she held on to my shoulders before hysterically laughing with me.

Tripp frowned and shook his head. "I wasn't ready for her Kung Fu grip."

Lina and I laughed harder. Tripp glared at us. Needing a moment, I headed for the kitchen sink and washed my hands. When my hands were clean of my indiscretion I walked back in the living room with a dishtowel in hand. My eyes landed on Shooter.

"Okay, can manwhore leave yet?" My whisper was loud and intentional. Irony. I was calling him a whore when minutes before I gave three tugs to his friend. Oh well it was still my place.

Lina nodded her head and stared Shooter dead on. "Yes. He said his peace."

Lina's face was set and I knew there was nothing in that moment Shooter could say that would change her mind.

"Darlin' we didn't even talk," Shooter's voice was soft and pleading.

"There is nothing more that needs to be said." Lina left no room for argument.

Tension filled the room. Needing my best friend to be fine I clapped my hands drawing attention to me. Shooter's eyes landed on me and I glared at him. "Out my house manwhore and take tug boat with you."

"It was the grip," Tripp yelled throwing his hands up in the air.

Patting Tripp's shoulder, I shoved him towards the door. "At least you have a big dick. That will get you somewhere in life even if you are three tugs."

Shooter looked over his shoulder as he walked out the door. "Catalina this isn't over darlin'. Not till I get you back."

Tripp was fighting me and I had to give him a few good shoves. "Out of here Tripp before I punch you again."

"I'm not leaving you with that first impression of me. I need as second chance to show you I'm worthwhile doll." His pleas were low but I'm sure Lina still heard him. Shaking my head "no" I shoved Tripp out the door. He turned to face me and I slammed the door in his face.

When I finally turned my attention to Lina she smiled but the humor was gone from her. "He wants me back."

"Of course he does." The guy wasn't an idiot, of course he realized what he lost.

Catalina stumbled on her words but finally spoke through her tears. "I hate him." She cried on my shoulder when I wrapped my arms around her. "He made me hate cherry lip gloss."

I didn't know how he made her hate cherry lipgloss but I was there for her as a friend should be. Holding her tighter I comforted her with one statement. "That bastard."

Chapter 2

~Tripp~

Funny thing. Thought I was going on this damn trip with Shooter, to get his girl back. What I wasn't expecting was this big titted, short, absolutely fucking gorgeous woman to answer the door. Her punch left me with a black eye but her Kung Fu grip on my cock left me wanting more than another hand job from her.

Shooter has this thing about love at first sight. Happened when he met Catalina. Thought he was a fool but laying in my hotel room thinking of a woman had me believing. Don't know if it was love, but it was something. I never thought of a girl like this. I was actually wondering if she would bail with me and we could go to the beach or something. I had two months and I wouldn't mind seeing her sexy ass in a bikini for that time before I convinced her to come on tour with me.

Fuck.

I think I had that shit. That love at first sight shit. Problem. I left her with a bad taste in her mouth and my first impression was crap. I needed a second chance. I needed to show her I was more than three tugs.

"Shooter, you up bro?" I called into the dark night. We had this cheap ass hotel close to Catalina's apartment building. The place was a shit hole, but had two beds and after touring in a bus it was not that bad.

"Fuck. I'm not going to sleep until she takes me back." Shooter answered me.

"The friend, do you know her name?"

"Crimson. She strips with Lina."

Crimson, that had to be a stage name. This girl was all fire. Fire red hair and fire temper and a good punch. Plus her grip was masterful and when she straddled her little body on top of mine those tits jiggled because they were real. All of that didn't belong to a Crimson. I was going to find out her real name then I was going to get my second chance with her.

"It happened to you, didn't it?" Shooter croaked out. "Love at first sight isn't bullshit."

Was I in love? I was in something that was for sure. "I think I just want to fuck her dude."

"Good luck tug."

"Call me that ever again or tell the guys and I'm gonna cut your throat while you sleep."

"Would be worth it though."

"It was her grip dude…Kung Fu."

Shooter just laughed at me.

Chapter 3

~Bella~

"You miss me yet?" I asked Maddox, my son, while I watered my plants that hung in my kitchen window.

"Not really," he laughed in to the phone.

Making puckering kissing sounds in to the phone, I laughed when he whined. The two of us were close and even though he hated me kissing or giving him hugs in public, he was still my baby. Spinning around to put the watering can under the sink where it belonged I jumped when I saw Tripp standing behind me.

"Baby I'll call you back later?" With an "okay" from Maddox I tossed my cell phone on the counter and placed a hand on my hip. "You breaking into my house now?"

Tripp crossed his arms over his chest. He was an impressive size and I wasn't talking just about the monster in his pants. Ripped with muscles that flexed when he moved, he was one of those rare males that had to have been born of the gods. However his prettiest feature next to his tattoos was his beautiful almost colorless gray eyes. I thought they were silver last night but in the daylight they were ever prettier. His silver eyes stood out beautifully against his lashes.

"Your door was open." Tripp moved past me and headed for my refrigerator. "Who were you talking to on the phone? Your boyfriend?"

Smirking I put the water can back under the sink and closed the refrigerator a second too late. Tripp twisted the cap off a beer and winked at me. "Why are you here? Lina isn't here."

"You're deflecting the question. You afraid to tell him you gave me a hand-job?"

At the mention of the hand-job I started laughing. The man had an impressive cock but he was a three-tug shooter. "For your own sake you shouldn't mention that story to anyone. Three tugs is not impressive."

Tripp downed his beer before slamming it onto the counter. His body was soon in my space as he crowded me and I backed against the counter. His long fingers wrapped around my hips and he lifted me onto the counter with him between my legs. Tripp unbuckled his spiked belt and unzipped his pants. My eyes drifted down and I wasn't surprised to see his hard cock pointing up at me. He really had the biggest dick I had ever seen and I kind of wanted to measure it. I had a ruler in the house somewhere.

Tripp took my hands and wrapped them around his velvet smooth length. "I think I can go longer than three tugs if you want you to test it out now. Last night was a fluke."

"Yo Tripp…dude put that shit away, you're in the middle of the kitchen." Shooter said walking in to *my* kitchen. Shooter looked at me holding Tripp's cock and then shook his head smiling. "Do you know where Lina is?" Shooter's voice was low and he had a small twang to it. Southern for sure but his look was far from any southern gentleman.

Trying to pry my hands from Tripp's cock, I gave up when he held my hands firmly in place. "At work and leave her alone, you cheating pussy eater."

Tripp laughed and Shooter smirked. With an arched brow Shooter questioned me. "Pussy eater?"

"Should I call you a cock sucker?"

"Pussy eater it is." Shooter winked at me then shook his head at Tripp. "Dude this one will eat you alive."

"I'm the one planning to do the eating," Tripp deadpanned.

"Don't fuck it up like me." Shooter left. Seconds later he slammed my front door shut.

"So where were we doll?"

"We were at the point where I tell you don't call me doll or any other nickname you give girls."

Tripp grinned at me and leaned in. His shaft thickened in my hands and became even harder. "What's your name then?"

"Isabella. Bella for short."

Tripp grinned. "Baby I don't do short," he moved my hands over his cock to drive his point home. "Well Isabella, you going to stroke my cock or are we just going to hang around your kitchen pretending that you don't want my cock in you."

Of course I wanted that impressive cock in me. I looked in Tripp's eyes, ignoring the bruising surrounding them. I might be short and mouthy but I had a punch to back up all my shit talk. I couldn't let him know how much I wanted that cock in me. There was a part of me that wanted him to think I was worth a little chase.

Why? I wasn't sure. It wasn't like this would be more than just a tumble in the sheets. All this was, was him wanting a second chance to show me his stamina.

"Sorry baby, but you don't meet the requirements to enter my pussy." I fluttered my lashes.

Tripp let go of my hands but I still kept them on his cock. I watched his hand travel up my legs. His tattooed fingers left a tingling hot trail against my skin and disappeared under my skirt out of view but I felt them creeping closer to my wet panties. His fingers ran across my mound, my panties the only thing blocking him from skin on skin contact. Squeezing his cock, I watched as he licked his lips. He flicked his fingers against my pussy and I hissed at the quick thump. On the counter I squirmed but Tripp's hands wouldn't allow me to squeeze my legs shut even if I needed to. And I needed to ease the pressure at my pussy.

"I think I meet every requirement," Tripp whispered in my ear. My hand sailed up and down his cock and he jerked his hips at the movement. "I think I'm the reason your pussy is soaking wet. Give me another chance and I'll show you how long my cock can last and what it can do to you."

My cell phone buzzed to life on the counter breaking the moment between. I let go of Tripp's cock and nudged him so I could get off the counter. He moved his hands from underneath my skirt and glared at my phone. The ring tone told me it was my son. With one hand Tripp pinned me in place and reached over picking up my phone. My heart started to thump. It was just a phone, but that phone was everything. Contacts, messages, and my son who was currently calling on it. My stomach sank as I bounced up to grab my phone, he held it out of reach. His eyes read the screen and seconds later my phone was at Tripp's ear. I punched his gut but he grunted, then used the one hand he had free to pin both of mine above my head against the cupboard. I struggled.

Tripp cleared his throat before speaking in to the phone. "Listen up cocksucker. Isabella is too busy sucking my cock right now and when she's is done, I'll be fucking her all day so just do us both a favor and don't call her back." Tripp's eyes widened.

Breath fled my body at Tripp's words. Horrified at what he just said I struggled with all my strength to get out of his hold. Those words, so rough and raw were spoken to my son. My eyes filled with tears as my heart skipped. Tripp looked down at me just as a tear fell down my face. Avoiding Tripp's face I looked down. His freed cock bounced between my legs hitting my thighs. A cock was out in the kitchen where I fed my son. I was the world's worst mother.

"Shit...hold on." Tripp stepped back releasing me. Handing me the phone, he turned around and shoved his cock back in his pants. I jumped off the counter.

"Mad, you there bud?" My voice quivered and my body shook with rage. What made me even madder at myself was the fact that my pussy was throbbing and my panties were uncomfortably wet.

Maddox breathed heavily in to the phone then his little childlike voice hit my ears. "Who's that mom?"

98

"An idiot."

Maddox laughed. My son was teetering between boy and man now. He knew what sex was. He asked me questions. He told me things that most mothers wished their children confided in them with. I never lied to my son when it came to sex. Hell, I was his age when I had him. I had to be open and honest to make sure he didn't make my mistakes. Although I would never say he was a mistake. He was my life and I would never change that.

"Mom is that your boyfriend?"

"No! He's just an idiot who thought it would be funny to answer my phone," I turned on my heels and punched Tripp in his gut again. He was expecting it because his stomach muscles flexed hard and I had to shake my hand out. God. Even that was sexy. Tripp's eyes were on me and I could almost say he was worried. "Did you need me bud?"

Maddox didn't answer me. With every breath in the phone my heart pounded. "I'll call you tomorrow mom."

"What was the reason you called?" I asked softly walking in to the living room. Tripp followed me and I flipped him off.

"It can wait mom." Maddox hung up on me without a good bye or I love you.

My fiery gazed landed on Tripp and he recoiled slightly. "I didn't know you had a kid."

"Look, whatever you came here for isn't going to happen." Heading to my door I pulled it open and pointed outside. "Next time you come to my house I expect you to knock or I'll call the cops."

Tripp nodded his head and headed towards the door. He paused in front of me. Light glinted off the metal of his eyebrow ring. Did he have an eyebrow ring last night? Whatever, it didn't matter I was pissed. "I'm really sorry. If I would have known it was a kid I wouldn't have said that shit. How old is your son?"

"Thirteen so he knows exactly what you just told him. Look. I understand you are a rock star and play bass or whatever but I'm not going to fuck you. I'm not a groupie and even though I gave you three tugs doesn't mean I'm easy. So just go find another girl to tug your meat 'cause I'm sure it won't be hard to find." I slammed my door in Tripp's face.

Chapter 4

~Tripp~

I took a page from Shooter's book. I fucked up. Worse, I cared that I fucked up. Before, if I offended a girl there was another to take her place. Before? Hell before was just a few days ago. I sat in the SUV in her driveway like a stalker. She didn't leave the house. I kept replaying what I did. That was her son on the phone, not some boyfriend.

Something had happened in that house with her. When I heard her on the phone, with what I thought was a guy, my mind fucking lost it. Hell I had tons of girls on me all the time. Part of the life style. I was lead guitarist of one the world's most famous metal bands. I showed up at a venue and pussy was handed to me. Some of the girls I've fucked had boyfriends, husbands, and it never bothered me before, but this girl had me all twisted. I was actually jealous. Jealous at the thought that she had a boyfriend. I knew she wasn't married because she had no ring on her pretty finger. At the thought of her fingers I groaned. My cock wanted them back on me.

Hell I just wanted this girl. And I wanted her for keeps.

I had already fucked this up majorly. Now I needed a second chance. Needed to redeem myself and my stamina. I ran a hand down my face formulating a plan.

Chapter 5

~Isabella~

This was the first summer that my son was away from me. My grandmother was enjoying his company and he was enjoying her pool. After Tripp left I had made a few calls to him. They went unanswered as did my texts. I hated the feeling that he was avoiding me.

After my shower I threw on a pair of sweats and a ratty tank top. I needed to calm my nerves so I headed to the backyard. The motion light kicked on and I nearly screamed. Tripp was sitting on my back patio table smoking a cigarette.

"What the hell are you doing?" I nearly screamed but remembered it was in the middle of the night and the neighbors were most likely sleeping.

"Knocked on your door but you didn't answer. Thought at first you were avoiding me so when I climbed in to your kitchen window I saw you were in the shower, I decided to come out here and smoke." His answer carried a bored tone to it. His cheeks sucked in as he inhaled from his cigarette. His chin lifted towards me. "Why you out here? Thought you'd be sleeping."

Heading to the grill, I lifted it up and pulled out a cigarette pack. "I'm a night owl due to my job. I thought I told you to get lost. Wait! Did you see me in the shower?"

Tripp pointed to the pack in my hands. "You smoke? It's not healthy for you."

"I'm quitting. Answer the question tug boat."

"I think we need to get this tug situation all settled. It was your grip. I think I can hold my own...now."

Laughing I put a cigarette between my lips and held my hand out for a lighter. Tripp handed me his and grinned. "I think you'll be holding it on your own for a while unless you find a willing girl who isn't me."

He smirked at me. His white teeth gleamed in the night. The upper half of Tripp's body was in darkness and the lower half in the porch light. I noticed his leather pants and biker boots. His black v-neck shirt was snug on his abs, though it had ridden up slightly exposing that low trail of hair that lead down in to his pants.

"You checking me out?" He asked lifting the hem of his shirt up exposing the muscled planes of his lower abdomen along with the colorful tattoos.

Not ashamed, I walked over and ran a hand up his stomach and nodded. His muscles tightened and the heat of his body radiated against my hand. I ran my fingers down his stomach following the happy trail just under his belly button and stopping at the fly of his leather pants. The beast in his pants twitched. Staring at his growing erection I traced it with my finger.

"So Isabella, you do know you are playing a dangerous game right?" His cigarette hung on the edge of his lips and his hands were gripping the arm of the patio chair he sat on. "I'm being real good now but you keep touching me I'm going to want to touch back."

What was I doing? Being stupid that's what I was doing. I palmed the head of his cock through his pants, then backed away puffing on my cigarette. He groaned and dropped his head back.

"Be sure to lock the back gate on your way out. I would hate for strange men to get in here." My eyes narrowed on him. Tossing my cigarette in to the flower pot I headed inside.

"You aren't going to invite me in?"

"No."

"Why?"

With a chuckle I opened the sliding door. "My first impression of you wasn't great."

"Give me a second chance to show you what I'm about."

Stepping inside the house I looked over to Tripp. He was very sexy but I knew where this ended. If Catalina was going to be with Shooter, which by the look in that boy's eyes I knew Lina wasn't going to have a chance at keeping him away, that meant I would have to see Tripp more often than I wanted to. It also meant sleeping with him was off the table. Complications were not my style. And of course there was the whole debacle of him speaking to my son. How could I forgive him for that?

"Have a good night lover boy." I closed the sliding door and locked it. The windows were then all closed and locked and for the first time in seven months, I actually armed my security alarm. Tripp laughed from the backyard.

From the sliding glass door I watched as Tripp came closer. He rested his hands on the glass and put his forehead against it. Crossing my arms over my chest I tilted my head to the side staring at him.

"Let me make it up to you. For the shit I said to your kid." His voice carried through the glass. Tripp pulled something out of his back pocket and slammed them against the glass. I stared at two plane tickets pressed against the glass. "Lina told me where your son was. Thought we could go visit him. I have to apologize to the kid."

Staring at plane tickets I blinked rapidly. Was this guy for real?

"What are you doing?" I asked trying to find his angle. "You doing this so I will sleep with you?"

Tripp shoved the tickets back in his pocket and shoved off the glass. "Trying to get a second chance here."

Against my better judgment I deactivated the alarm and unlatched the sliding glass door. Tripp smiled as he stepped through and his smile got bigger when I closed the door and locked it behind him. Taking an annoyed breath, I spun around to face the blue haired devil. That's when I noticed it for the first time. Out in the dark I couldn't tell but here under the soft light of the kitchen it was clear, his blue hair was gone. Instead, it was dark brown.

Tripp smirked and held out his hand. I looked at it for a minute before taking it. He shook my hand, "Tripp Rivers."

"Isabella Vega."

Tripp lifted my hand to his lips and kissed my hand. Tossing my head back in laughter, I playfully pushed him and took my hand back. He grinned at me and pulled the plane tickets out of his back pocket. I took them inspecting them. First class. I didn't need to know how he got my information, I was sure Lina told him. I'm sure it was payback from the time I drove Shooter to her apartment.

"We leave in the morning, and Lina took care of your hours at the club." Tripp leaned against the counter and crossed his ankles and arms staring at me. "Changed my hair to look more responsible and I'm going to make it up to your kid. Tell him I was stupid and maybe buy his forgiveness. Thirteen right? I'm pretty sure I can buy his forgiveness."

The gesture was sweet but it wasn't happening. "I can't accept this Tripp."

Tripp moved forward and I moved back until my ass was against the counter. He placed a hand on each side of my body, leaning in to the counter and me. His mouth was close and I tried to ignore it. It was hard though since I knew what his mouth tasted like and how he kissed. My body tingled with goose bumps and my stomach did that floppy thing.

"Why?" He asked. His voice sent chills down my body and I squeezed my thighs together. He was affecting me in ways he shouldn't. Not for a guy who I really didn't know.

Placing a hand on his chest, I pushed him back but he didn't budge so my hand just stayed on his warm chest. "I don't think it's a good idea for you to meet him. First of all he loves your band and second it would give him the wrong impression about us."

Tripp pushed off the counter and backed up from me. The space between us was cold and in that moment I realized I liked him in my space. I liked that floppy feeling in my stomach and the warm air that surrounded him.

Tripp ran a hand down his face and nodded his head. "When we go I will stay at the hotel. You can't say no because this is part of my second chance you are giving me."

"Oh really? And what's the other part?"

"Where I show you I'm more than three tugs." He didn't smile but met me with challenging eyes.

He placed the plane tickets down on the counter. My head turned to watch him but I froze when his hand slid around my neck and under my hair. He pulled me towards him, our lips smashed together and his teeth raked across my lips painfully. The pain was replaced with lust as his tongue found its way in to my mouth.

His upper body curved and folded over mine, wrapping me in his strong arms. My arms moved under his and up his back until my hands grasped his shoulders. Our mouths danced and tongues fought as our bodies slowly moved together.

His strong hands moved down my back and cupped my ass. I danced on poles for a living so there was no strained effort as I pulled myself up his body and wrapped my legs around his waist. Tripp's hands went from my ass to the back of my thighs and without breaking our kiss he carried me down the hallway, while I ground against his cock.

Tripp's tongue slid against mine and my hips moved against his. I could feel his cock hardening and my pussy clenched in anticipation. There was a faint moment of regret that bristled in the back of my mind but I pushed it aside. Sometimes sexual needs trumped logic. This was one of those cases. I was enticed by Tripp. There was no denying I wanted his cock and I would sort the morals out in the morning when I gave him the plane tickets back.

My back hit my bed and Tripp shoved my legs apart before resting between them. He ground his leather covered shaft against my needy core. Grabbing his hair I pulled back his head removing his lips from mine. With his head tilted I kissed down his neck and used one hand to shove him off of me. We flipped over smoothly and he was on his back and I was straddling his torso. My mouth trailed down his neck while my hands pushed up his shirt. Tripp yanked the material and pulled it up and over his head tossing it across the room. His grey, heated eyes watched as I started to trail down his chest licking and kissing. His tattoos moved as he flexed and breathed heavily.

"Get yourself mentally ready tug boat." I smiled up at him as I started unbuttoning his leather pants.

Tripp put his hands behind his head and looked down at me like he was relaxed. "I'm ready Kung Fu grip."

With one yank of his leather pants, Tripp's swollen, erect cock released from its confines. On my knees I leaned back allowing his shaft to bob in my direction. He was the biggest guy I had ever seen and I was turned on at the thought of his dick entering me. That was if we could get past three tugs.

My left hand wrapped around the base of his shaft and my right hand moved towards the top of the monstrous appendage. Before this night was done, we were measuring his shit. My hands in sync, I moved them up his shaft tightening my grip. He throbbed and thickened even more. I ran my thumb over the sensitive head and toyed with his piercing. He bit his lower lip and tensed. I looked up at him and smirked. That was one tug.

Biting my lower lip I moved my hand down his cock twisting my hands as I brought them back up his shaft. This time when I reached the top of his cock I used my flattened tongue to run across the head. Tripp moved his hips, thrusting upwards. That was tug number two.

His breathing was heavier as he glared down at me. "That was cheating."

Flicking out my tongue I ran it across his piercing moving the barbell back and forth. Tripp groaned. Flattening my tongue once again I ran it down his length and across the top of his heavy sack. Tripp jerked his hips up. Satisfied with the reaction I ran my tongue back up his length. Normally toying with a guy's knob was not at the top of my list but Tripp's small reactions made me want to never stop. Every response he gave drenched my panties. Angling my mouth I opened wider and took the head of his cock in between my lips, sucking hard before popping it out. I think that counted as tug number three.

He grunted.

"So I should stop?" My voice was thick.

Tripp grabbed the back of my head. His long fingers twined in my hair possessively. Maneuvering his hips he brought my lips back to his cock. I opened my mouth and took him in. He guided me down his length. I took as much as I could and used my hands to pump the bottom of his shaft where I could not reach. Swirling my tongue around his dick I sucked hard and moved quickly up and down his beautiful cock. I popped the crown of his shaft from my mouth again and gave one last final pumping tug with my hands. He gritted his teeth but didn't blow.

"No stopping." Tripp groaned out.

He moved his hands over mine. In hard fast movements he guided my hands up and down his dick. Alternating my grip, I flicked my tongue flicked out catching the head of his cock. Tripp let go of my hands and gripped me under my arms. Showing power I didn't realize he had, he tossed me on the bed. His hands roughly moved down my body cupping and squeezing my breasts before moving to my sweats. His fingers hitched under the top of my sweats, hooking my lace panties in his grasp. He placed a kiss on my stomach where my shirt rode up as he yanked my sweats and panties off.

Air hit my wet pussy causing me to whimper.

"You better not hold back on me doll. I want you screaming out my name," Tripp growled out.

Lifting my head up, braced on my elbows looking directly in to those silver eyes. "Do I look like I'm a screamer?"

Tripp smirked but didn't answer me. When he pushed my thighs apart and ran his hot tongue down my slit I gasped arching off the bed.

How did I miss the fact he had a pierced tongue?

More importantly, how did I not know I was a screamer?

Chapter 6

~Tripp~

Fuck Shooter and his love at first sight.

It was love at first fucking taste!

Going down on a woman was never something I had to do. Fuck I had women wanting my cock, not the other way around. But the moment her mouth was on me working me over, I wanted to reciprocate. I wanted to taste her, suck her clit and fuck her with my fingers before I shoved my large cock in her tight body. I wanted to know every inch of her body.

My tongue moved through her wet folds toying at her entrance before circling her clit. I pressed my tongue ring at her entrance fucking her with it until her hands grappled for the sheets. Her wetness drenched my face and I licked it up like a champ. I wanted her pretty pussy to cum all over me. I wanted to hear Isabella scream my name as she lost control.

Looking up at her from her perfect thighs I smirked. "I knew you'd be perfection."

Not giving her a moment to retort I dipped my head down to her waiting core. Clamping my mouth around her clit, I sucked while I moved my fingers deep inside of her. Turning my fingers I pumped two of them in and out of her tight entrance. She squeezed her walls around my digits and I curled them hitting that spot deep in her. Isabella squeezed her thighs around my head moaning. Her soft moans egged me on. Frantically flicking my tongue over her swollen bud, I pounded my fingers in her harder.

Isabella was perfection. Every moment she made was art to my eyes. Her hips raised from the bed as she ground against my face. Her slender fingers moved down her body until they ran through my hair. Her tits heaved with each one of her ragged breaths. Her bottom lip was trapped between her teeth, but when she couldn't contain herself anymore her head fell back and her mouth formed a perfect "O". Her hands moved from my hair and fisted in the sheets. Isabella's back arched further from the bed.

My cock dripped and throbbed wanting attention.

"Fuck!" She softly gasped as her hands released their grip on the sheets.

My tongue lazily ran up her slit as I watched Isabella grab her own tits. Against her clit I groaned, gazing at her perfect body as she pulled on her own nipples. Sexy. She wasn't shy about it; she rolled her nipples between her manicured fingers. I wanted them in my mouth. Sucking hard on her clit, my eyes stayed on her as she ground against my face. My free hand moved to her tits and I kneaded them. They were big and real and I loved how my tattooed hand looked against her tan skin. A streak of jealousy hit when I remembered other men saw these tits on a regular basis.

It was then my murky heart pumped to life. I was going to make this girl mine!

A fourth finger entered her tight pussy and she came. Thrashing. My fingers continued to pump within her until she relaxed onto the bed. With one last kiss to her perfect pussy I flipped Isabella over on her stomach. With my help she moved, pushing her perfect round ass in to the air. Running my fingers through her again I held my cock in one hand.

"This is gonna hurt doll." I warned. I wasn't stupid. My shit was big and most girls couldn't take it all in.

"Don't call me doll," her voice was muffled in the pillow.

Grinning I placed my dick at her entrance. My piercing moved sending a flash of pleasure up my spine. My balls tightened. I wasn't prepared for Isabella to push back against me. We both cried out as she impaled herself with my cock. I was balls deep in her and she clenched my shit like a vice.

I was in love with this girl.

Chapter 8

~Isabella~

His cock was in me, throbbing and filling me in all directions. Painfully he pushed in a little more and it hit deep. The balls of his piercing scored inside my body bringing another orgasm close to the surface.

Tripp grabbed my hips and a gasp pulled from me as he slid out then drove back in me. "We were built for each other." He grunted out.

My head bobbed up and down in agreement. Puzzle pieces fit together, Tripp and I melded together. His cock in me and my pussy clutching him, there was no better completion. "I never thought I would agree with you."

His laughter filled the room and I bucked back against him driving his cock into me. Tripp's hands moved up my back until his hand tangled in my hair. He used my hair for leverage as he pistoned his hips. "There is no fucking disagreeing about how you were made for me."

He was right.

His balls bounced against my body and I whimpered at the contact. His colossal pulsating cock glided in and out of me. My walls clamped, gripping him. The friction between our bodies built. My tits ached and bounced with his thrusts.

"On your knees and wrap your arms around my neck," Tripp ordered as he slapped my ass. The sting of his slap subsided when his palm hit my other ass cheek.

Shakily I moved up to my knees. Tripp's cock was still buried in me. My hands moved up and behind until my arms were secure around his neck. My back was lined with his front and my legs wrapped backwards around his thighs. I couldn't hold this position long, but that fear left when he grabbed my thighs supporting my weight. With a grunt Tripp adjusted me up his cock. He held my body weight, moving me up and down. He was bouncing my pussy up and down his cock. My tits bounced with his pace. The bulbous tip of his cock hit my G-spot with each move. My arms shook and I moved my hips trying to ride him harder.

"I want to fuck you harder." He gritted in my ear.

I moaned out his name. He let go of me and I crashed down on to the bed on all fours. Tripp pulled my hair back until my head was upwards and my neck was arched and exposed. Leaning over my body, he pulled his cock out. The pierced head of his dick moved through my folds and pushed at my sensitive clit. Bucking back I rubbed my clit against his head. He grunted and moved his cock head over my clit again. We moved in circular motions teasing each other. Tripp's mouth landed on my bare shoulder and he kissed it tenderly just before he shoved his cock deep in to me. I didn't have time to adjust to the length and fullness. He pulled out before barreling in to me again. My legs trembled and he pulled on my hair keeping me up. The tingling of pain at my scalp dissipated when he started to piston in and out of me. The bed rocked and our bodies slapped hard against one another. Every slide and pump built a friction that was leading to orgasm.

Taking my hand I moved it down my body until I found my clit, one flick sent a pulsating wave a pleasure through me. Playing with myself, I moved my hips back and forth meeting Tripp's thrusts.

"Harder," my voice projected between my gritted teeth.

Tripp pulled on my hair, forcing me to arch my back. "Can you handle harder?"

Our bodies collided together. The sound bounced off the walls. The drum beat of our bodies slapping together increased. Tripp held on to me tight as he slammed repetitively in to me.

"Fuck me Tripp," I screamed out absorbing every thrust he drove into me.

My fingers trembled around my clit. Tripp let go of my hair and held on to my hips. Small tremors trickled through my body, my orgasm was within reach. His hand ran down my back tenderly. My body slightly stiffened when he shoved his finger in my ass. There was no hesitation in me when Tripp's finger and cock moved in similar rhythms. My fingers toyed with my clit in the same tempo as Tripp. All the sensations were too much.

"Tripp!" My throat burned as I screamed out his name.

Tripp moved his hips, gliding his dick in and out of me until he groaned leaning over me. Hot cum filled me. He removed his finger from my ass and my orgasm kicked back up. Tripp held on to me as I became boneless in his arms. His cock drove into me one last time. He buried his jerking cock deep inside, keeping us joined as we both fell on to the bed.

Between his panting breaths Tripp placed soft kisses across my back.

"I don't think I can call you tug anymore," I panted into the pillow.

Tripp laughed, his cock twitching in me. "A second chance was all I needed to make the right impression."

The bed dipped and his weight left my body. When he pulled out I whimpered at the loss. My body was raw and aching in ways I hadn't experienced before. The cold air ran across my skin and I lifted my head to find the man that was missing from the bed. Tripp's ass disappeared in to the bathroom. A moment later he emerged from the bathroom with a wash cloth in hand.

Flipping on to my back I sat up as he kneeled on to the bed. Tripp parted my legs and ran the warm cloth across my throbbing pussy. The look on his face darkened as he glanced up my sweaty body. I swore I saw a flash in those silver eyes.

His tongue ran across his lips as he tossed the washcloth aside. Moving over my body Tripp rested his hips between my thighs. His weight was deliciously on top of me, and it felt right. His head lowered until his lips brushed mine.

"Do you believe in love at first sight?"

I didn't know how to answer him, but I didn't have to. He pressed his lips against mine and our tongues collided.

In the morning, I was going to take him up on his offer with the plane ticket. I wouldn't introduce him to Maddox but I would get to know this guy. Something told me he deserved a chance. However Tripp Rivers would only get one chance at my heart.

WICKED GAME

By Josephine Ballowe

Two weeks ago a client asked if he could eat me. I don't mean eat me in the *shove your face fiercely between my thighs* manner or *forcing his tongue deep inside me and licking me until I scream with pleasure* sort of way.

No, not like that at all. He meant to eat me, with his teeth and jaws type of way – working his way from my fingers, up my arms, swallowing me whole kind of way. That fellow I knew was crazy and I left him right where I found him. As if I won't need my skin anytime soon.

I'm not a judgmental person. I've been on my own since I was 17 – making my way however I could. I've had clients want to play vampires before, I've had men and women tie me up and spank me. I will say that by far the worst role-play was dressing up like a Victorian nanny while the CEO of large New York department store sucked my nipples while he wore a diaper. You don't think that sounds so bad? Well, he peed in it too and *I* had to change him.

I've done all of this with no complaints and I've done things most people would never understand. But I believe there is a need for people like me. I keep marriages together and keep men sane. Really, I do. Without me, wives would have to play these games – and if they didn't they'd have very discontented husbands on their hands. And that is never a good thing. I provide security and connubial bliss around the Big Apple – a necessary outlet for whatever scratches your itch. In fact, doing the most perverted acts is how I make my money – and pretty good money at that.

Last night an older gentleman with an upper class accent wanted me to meet him at bar in a rougher part of the city. His request was that I only to wear a knee length red coat – yes indeed, he specified the color red – and nothing else underneath. He also requested that I have at least "a moderate amount of pubic hair". I guess the old guy was old school, I don't know. Lucky for him I was late for my Brazilian.

I caught a cab to the bar, fully nude under my coat as requested. He called my cell phone as the cab pulled up and insisted I unbutton the coat. I was to "inadvertently" flash the patrons then shower him with attention and occasionally expose myself. Sounds simple, right? In my business, my priority is to do whatever the client likes and wherever they want it done. Flashing a few drunks was easy money for sure.

He was easily recognizable; he wore an ascot for fuck's sake. This guy had slicked back hair and shiny black shoes and looked very uptight and particular. Easy money, I kept saying to myself, easy money.

I breezed through the circular door, unbuttoned, nude, and hairier than I'd like my pussy to be. The room was chilled, the breeze from the door blew open my red coat and a few men noticed the pale skin of my breasts peaking from under my coat. I don't have big breasts, but I like them small. To be honest, men don't care about the size – they think they do but I've had enough threesomes to know they like the natural feel far more than giant saline bubbles stitched under your skin.

Like a gentleman, he rose to greet me and direct me to the table. Or so I thought. "Don't speak," he instructs with his stilted and strange voice. Though he must be older than my father, I find his voice stimulating. His hand reached under my coat and cupped my breast. His breath was hot and sweet.

He rolled my nipples between his fingers and pinched them as we walked to the table. It will take way more than that if he wants to make me flinch. As we are stood near the bar, one of the pool players looks at me, intrigued by our little public sex game. My nipples became so firm that I was surprised they didn't rip their way from under my coat. I look at the smiling bartender and feel my pussy dampen and moved my client's hand from my nipples down to my cunt. I push myself against him, rubbing myself against his hand. He withdrew immediately.

"I won't touch that now," he said.

"What do you mean by 'that'?" I answered, somewhat offended.

He kept silent but led me to the backstairs by my nipples. A low growl comes from his throat. I must be crazy – what kind of man can growl like an animal? "Downstairs," was all he muttered in a guttural deep voice.

"Wonderful," I answer. I mean, whatever floats your boat.

As we descended the stairs, a strange thumping music assaulted my body. The low bass changed the rhythm of my heart – this wasn't ordinary techno music. This was something eerie, like the music from a horror movie.

As soon as my eyes adjusted to the light, I saw men and women in various state of arousal. A young raven-haired woman was chained to an iron table; her nipples were being sucked by two older women dressed in crimson robes on either side of her. Between her legs was a man pounding into her with such force I thought the chains would break. But none of that freaked me out. What freaked the shit out of me were the bags of blood hanging from the ceiling in IV bags. The man whose cock was pounding the girl's pussy right out from under her was drinking the blood from a tube as he moved. He was greedy, gulping and sucking like an animal. I think the blood turned him on more than the girl.

"What is going on here?" I calmly asked my client. I remained calm because rule number one in my business was to never seem afraid.

"Don't worry, I won't hurt you," he answered. I looked around the room at the whips and tethers. "They won't hurt you either," he added. "But, I would ask that you take your coat off now. This is for pleasure."

"For pleasure?"

"Yes, our master's pleasure. The leader of our demonic race. The One we follow before all others."

"I've had enough," I stated. "Nothing in our agreement stated anything about 'demonic races' – I don't play that rough, usually. At least not the first time."

"Lisbette," he began, "there can be no agreement between me and you, for you are one of us."

"What? Who the hell is Lisbette? My name is Elizabeth, asshole."

"Perhaps that is what you were told as a child. Perhaps that is what everyone on earth calls you and perhaps that is what you believe. But what you are is a succubus. And I am privileged to be the one who brought you home."

"Okay," I said, as I got more and more irritated. "If we are going to play this succubus game and drink this obviously fake blood, your evening is going to cost a lot more!"

"This is no game, Lisbette. This is who we are. This is who you are. Now you have been found and returned to us."

"Listen!" I screamed. "I've been in sex dens before, none of this shocks me," I lied. "But we need to renegotiate our financial arrangement ASAP or I'm out of here."

"Lisbette," he growled. His voice rumbled deep inside his chest. "You will stay. There is no 'out of here'. You are here now, you are one with us. And finally, there is no arrangement."

A redhead approached me with a pair of latex panties. "Here, Malcolm." She never met his eyes. "These are for her."

Malcolm's eyes widened as he saw that on the inside were not one, but two heavy rubber dildos. He watched as Persephone

124

poured lube all over the dildos and pointed for me to step into them. She pulled them up for me, sliding one into my cunt and the other into my ass. I gasped as the dildos settled into place, I felt filled to the limit. Next she pulled out a metal bar, three feet long with shackles on the end. She looked at Malcolm for his approval and he nodded. At that point it sounded silly to call him client, I didn't know if this was a game or if it was real life.

Persephone expertly buckled my legs into them, leaving them spread as wide as they would go. Then I was led to a wooden table and ordered to lie down.

"Now," he whispered as a small crowd of masked onlookers gathered around. One man was stroking another man's cock as I lay on a wooden table. Persephone began to suck on Malcolm's hard cock. Her hands reached behind and she spread his ass cheeks, gently fingering his asshole. When Malcolm was about to climax, staring down at me with my legs spread, Persephone stopped sucking and fingering him.

"This is what the we have been waiting for." She brought out a large whip, four feet long of plaited leather, and let it trail lazily behind her. In a flash of ecstasy she forced the handle of the whip into her pussy. She climbed onto the table and stepped into the large space between my legs. She situated herself between my legs and began grinding against my latex panties, shoving the dildos in further as she rode me scissor style.

"Get off her, Persephone. Stand back," demanded Malcolm. "You've never had this before, have you?" I realized his voice was not so much upper class Bostonian but more Satanic – deep and low.

I shook my head wildly. Truth is, I have been whipped before and it's no big deal. But, I had always been in control before. With this group, I had no idea what to expect.

Persephone pulled my hair and tied a gag ball into my mouth. I began to bite down on the gag with anticipation. The sight of men and women watching me turned me on beyond belief. I never thought I was an exhibitionist, and I thought I had done it all. I was ridiculously wrong about that.

I tried to squeeze my legs back together but the bar kept them far apart. I didn't know whether to fight or to enjoy.

Malcolm smiled as Persephone's breasts swung side to side, a heavy chain pulled on her nipples. His face showed his pleasure in knowing he could do absolutely anything to anyone.

Persephone took the whip from her wet pussy and passed it to Malcolm. He cracked the whip inches away from my thighs, close enough that I felt the air move around me.

Persephone grabbed the whip from him. "Let me show her how this works."

I was pulled from the table and placed in front of it.

Fucking A, I thought. Now some psycho bitch is going to whip me. And guess what? She did. She left a harsh red stripe across the lower part of my backside. I jumped, I had played with many whips before but this one was different – it left a cooling sensation

126

not a harsh pain, and also the marks faded quickly with immense pleasure.

Malcolm touched my ass. "Lisbette…you are truly her…" He touched the fading welt and kissed it, feeling the slightly raised skin on his tongue. I twitched under his touch, surprised how much I enjoyed this. A woman to my right began to orgasm as a short demon licked her pussy, nibbling her clit – sucking it into his mouth and then releasing it. Her orgasm brought a shower of cum across my arm. Malcolm raised the whip again; my ass shook underneath me waiting for the moment of pain and release. He quickly snapped the whip right where the dildo was entering my pussy. I cried out with pleasure. Believe me, yelling in pleasure is very unusual. I am usually a pretty quiet fuck.

I felt energized and alive – I was on sensory overload. Malcolm pressed his stiff cock against my ass, he leaned over and his chest was hard against my back. I looked at him over my shoulder and saw guilt cross his face but I managed to nod and barely smile to show him it didn't matter. I was too wrapped up in my own pleasure.

Malcolm stepped away from me and grabbed another whip from the floor. This one caused me some alarm as it looked like a six-foot long black-as-night snake. This time he swung upwards so that the leather flew between my thighs and across my labia, just hard enough for me to muffle a moan.

Malcolm stroked my face. "You're loving this now, aren't you?" he whispered into the back of my neck. The heat from his breath and the heat from room had me in a huge sweat. My hair was wet, my thighs, and my stomach - not to mention my pussy.

Persephone pushed him away from me and fell to her knees, taking him deeply into her mouth again. She licked his cock up and down and messaged his balls. Next she began to stroke herself, faster and faster. I could do nothing but watch her bring Malcolm to the brink. I looked at him and into his eyes – something was familiar, some connection.

"Now, finish it," Persephone ordered.

"You do not order me around," Malcolm yelled. His voice rose and echoed through the room. Again, there was something familiar in his voice.

Persephone knelt again and began to lick his balls as Malcolm unbuckled my legs from the spreader bar. I was hypnotized and completely under his control. Hell, I enjoyed this so much I should probably pay him.

I tried to stand but I clung limply to the table. Malcolm pulled the latex panties down as he kicked Persephone away from him. Juices ran down my thighs as Malcolm picked my legs up and wrapped them around his hips. Holding me by the ass, he slammed his cock deep into my soaking cunt, grinding my clit. For a moment, he became motionless, allowing me to relish the sensation of him inside me. Then I twitched.

Behind me was Persephone! Would she not go away? I looked over my shoulder to see her with a huge black strap on. She gently pressed it into my ass. Slowly she slid it deeper and deeper in as Malcolm fucked my dripping pussy. He smiled as he could feel the strap on pumping inside me, adding to his pleasure also.

I bucked and writhed uncontrollably as Malcolm and Persephone slammed me from both directions. The "audience" was a mixture captivated sex fiends mixed with indifferent, more intellectual types. One woman, dressed in black with a flaming red scarf with lipstick to match, walked over. She was slender and pale. Her hair was pinned into a tight chignon.

She stared into my eyes; hers were a mixture of yellow and brown – like a tiger's eye. I knew her from somewhere. I have seen her walking the streets of New York many times out of the corner of my eye.

"I want to hear you," she said. "Then I will know for sure." She pulled the ropes that held the gag in placed and tossed it to the floor. My lips felt stretched and dry. She brushed my hair back and put her red lipstick on me to moisten my lips. "Speak."

I let out a deep primal scream of pleasure as I came, over and over again, squirting all over Malcolm with an immense flood of juice.

Malcolm arched his back as his hot semen filled me to the core. He clung to me, soaked in sweat as he finished his last few strokes and collapsed on top me, pressing me to the cold table.

The beautiful woman still stared. "Yes, she is Lisbette. Our own Jezebel. I delivered you into this world." I couldn't believe it. She looked far to young to have delivered me.

She read my mind. "I do not age. Nor will you from this point on. You are home."

"What?" I reacted with shock. "Game is over now, people. Back to reality and to settle up."

"I like her more than I'd thought."

"Shut up, Magda," instructed Malcolm as he wiped himself with a towel and dressed. I looked at him and this man of 60 years was suddenly a man of 30. "A disguise," he told me. "It would be more believable if a more mature gentleman wanted your very unique services."

I felt faint as their words absorbed into my thoughts. I looked around the room to very familiar faces. Faces that had followed me around the city for years.

"We did follow you," said Magda as she read my mind and saw the confusion in my face. "But only to be sure it was you. We lost you when you were a child and we didn't want to bring the wrong succubus back to us."

"How did you lose me? My parents are alive and in Brooklyn?"

"No. Your father is Satan. Your mother is, well, truly your mother. She agreed to bear you but she but took you from us against her contracted agreement. We couldn't find her. But we knew we were getting close when we saw you."

"So this fuckfest was for nothing?"

"No," said the younger looking Malcolm. "This is how we live. How we survive."

130

"What about the bags of blood on the wall?"

"Some of us drink it," said Magda matter of factly. "It keeps us strong. We steal it from the hospital or we get it…naturally at its source."

"Great…vampire demons?"

"You will meet your father soon," interrupted Magda. "You have demonic strength with human logic – an interesting combination."

As she spoke I felt my lower jaw move, I felt thirsty, my teeth felt tight.

"Give her some blood! Quickly!" Persephone yelled. "She is hungry."

"No!" I yelled. "I don't drink blood."

Malcolm filled a cup with blood. "With your realization and acceptance will come your demonic desires. You are unable to fight them now that you know the truth. Drink this." He forced my mouth open and the warmth and thickness of the blood soothed me.

My coat was pooled at the floor, covered in cum. Ruined, completely ruined.

"Go ahead and put it on. Try to leave. Once you have the knowledge, it can't be undone. Just ask Eve." She pointed to a lovely woman sitting sadly in a darkened corner on a satin covered settee.

Concentrating hard, I grabbed my coat. Suddenly the outside light was too bright. I had no appetite but I wanted the blood from those bags more than anything. I felt more pleasure centered between my legs. Everyone smiled. Every inch, every molecule, every pore of my body was on fire. Magda passed me a crimson velvet gown. It fit perfectly and I knew I would never leave. This is who I was, a succubus, born of the devil.

I walked to where Eve sat, still and unmoving. I looked down at her. She looked back at me with the blackest eyes I have ever seen. "See? Once you seek truth and knowledge you can never go back. Welcome to Hell."

ONE MORE ROUND

By Caroline Baker

Come on, Baby

Let's play a game

Try to find out

If we really feel the same

We'll each roll the dice

Banking on luck

Hoping somehow

We don't fuck it up

I'll go all in

You can fold

And we'll see how long

We can both hold

On to the reasons

We felt like we'd win

When we decided

To play again

Two worthy players
Who've both lost before
Hoping that this time
Fate settles the score

You leave the table
To take a smoke break
Calm your nerves
Review what's at stake

I'll just stay put
And pray for the best
Hope that my high cards
Can cover the rest

You're thinking back
To plays gone awry
Lessons you learned
That you now can apply

I'm thinking how much
I learned at the end
And what I'd do different
If we played again

Waiting to see

If you had as much fun

Or if you're just ready

To pack up and be done

Cause you play the odds

While I bank on fate

But I realize

It's getting pretty late

And you may not

Be returning at all

But just in case

I'll give you until last call

Cause I'm feeling lucky

Up for one more game

And I'm hoping that you

Feel exactly the same

Facing the Past

By Sabina Bundgaard

The memory flashed before her eyes while driving the car back home. It was a rental so she didn't have to worry about returning it back to Copenhagen once she was done. She just had to find the local office and drop it off.

A single tear escaped the corner of her eye, making its way down her cheek. Irritated, she wiped it away with her hand, cursing under her breath.

Driving normally relaxed her, but tonight everything was churning inside her head. Random thoughts jumped forth, making her alternate between wincing at her stupidity and cursing him. How could she be so blind? She should've guessed with all the late nights, cancelled dinners - love truly made you blind.

"Adam isn't worth it Emily," she said to herself. "Don't waste your tears on him." Checking her rearview mirror before signaling her turn, Emily sighed in relief. Almost home now. She couldn't wait to be surrounded by her friends and family again, it'd been too long since she saw them last. Adam was always so busy and required her to be there for him when he was at different outings that bored her to death every single time. She hated getting all dressed up for no reason, other than to be paraded in front of his associates.

Making a face at the memory of the last party where he actually scolded her like a child for snapping at one of his bosses for grabbing her ass. Heat rose to her cheeks at the mere memory and she could still feel the anger and shame lurking right underneath the surface. Shaking it off, Emily took another turn, getting closer to her parents old house. Driving down the old roads, serenity washed over her, making her loosen the deathgrip she had on the steering wheel since she left home.

The darkness made the last turn a bit harder to see, and Emily slowed down so she wouldn't miss it.

"Where are you, where are you?" Mumbling to herself, Emily slowed the car down to a snail pace until she finally recognized the old driveway. For ages her father have been talking about getting it fixed, to put some lights up, but it never happened. It had become a standard comment in the family to joke about it as the first thing when someone walked through the door.

With a sigh of relief Emily parked the car in front of the house. For a moment she just sat there, staring at it, letting old memories wash over her. Memories from a happier time. When the front door in the house opened and the warm light from inside the house spilled out, Emily snapped out of it, automatically plastered a smile on her lips before opening the car door. She could hear her mother yelling at her dad.

"I told you someone was in the driveway! Now get out here before I make you!" The smile that spread over Emily's face was real, although tinged with sadness. She missed her family, her old friends.

"It's just me mom."

"Emily?" Her mother squinted her eyes to better see into the darkness, and a broad smile spread when she saw it was indeed her only daughter. "What are you doing here? Why are you driving that car? Where's Adam?"

"I hope you left that useless piece of... Ugh." Her father's last word got cut off when her mom elbowed him in the stomach. Rubbing the sore spot, he gave his wife a glare. Emily didn't respond immediately, but gave her mother a hug and leaned in to give her dad a peck on the cheek. Her dad's hair is almost gray, only small patches of black is still visible, but his green eyes were alert as always, looking behind her, waiting for her husband to arrive from the shadows. When a minute passed and he still hadn't made his appearance, she could see his wheels turning, and the million dollar question jumped into his eyes. Silently, Emily shook her head, making her black curls bounce a little around her. Her hair and eye color she got from her dad, but the curls? All courtesy of her mother.

"Why don't you come in and we'll make a cup of tea, hmm? I'm sure you've had an eventful day. Do you have more bags in the car?"

Shaking her head, Emily followed her parents inside the house, carefully closing the door behind her, shutting off her previous life.

***

"He did what?!" Her father's outrage was clear, Emily wondered if their neighbors would be calling anytime soon to check up on them.

"Daddy, please. Sit down."

"I always knew he was trouble. I should've…"

"What is done is done, Jens. You can't change it now." Her mother turned toward her, looked directly at her daughter before she asked, "Are you going to forgive him and go back to him? You know he's been good to you, darling."

Surprise smacked directly into Emily like freight train, leaving her speechless. Her mother sat there, looking at her expectantly, her blue eyes shining, her head tilted to the side, making her blond curls tip.

"Lisa, you don't mean that!" Her dad's indignation woke Emily from her stupor. Shaking her head to clear her thoughts, Emily looked at her mom.

"No. He cheated on me. Not once, but several times, with different women. I'm not taking him back. If he can't even respect me to not cheat on me, then what if. No mom. I'm filing for divorce as soon as I can. End of story. Now if you don't mind, I'm going to bed." Her mom's face fell as she told her off, but quickly recovered.

Her dad followed her to the stairs to help her find the different blankets and what not before she got to bed.

"Don't mind you mother, Ems. She's a hopeless romantic. Lord knows I love her for it, but reality isn't always picture perfect. You're doing the right thing. I never thought he was good enough for you anyway." He gave her a hug. His last words were spoken into her hair, so they got a bit muffled, but the meaning was clear.

"Thank you daddy. I have to go see the lawyer tomorrow to get everything sorted out though."

"I'll drive you myself. Now go get some sleep, you must be tired by now."

***

The drive into town didn't take long and Emily enjoyed the peace and quiet in the car. Her dad never minced words, that day was no exception. Her mother had desperately tried to talk her out of it during breakfast but Emily was determined. No matter what happened she was going to go through with it. There were things that she hadn't told her parents and, even though she loved them dearly, she didn't want to lay it on them.

Stepping into the lawyer's office was surreal. Emily shivered a little in the airconditioned room and suddenly she wished that she had taken her coat with her. Her dad was already at the receptionist's desk, talking to the pretty brunette sitting there. Looking around, it seemed like a normal office – heaven knows she seen her fair share of them.

"Emily?" The male voice made her turn around in surprise. Her breath caught in her throat. In the other end of the reception was Janus, her old friend from school. He's in a dark suit, his brown hair messy like he just ran his hand through, his dark blue eyes twinkling, and his smile.

Oye, was she in trouble. Janus was her best male friend back in school and she had always had a secret crush on him.

"J..Janus? What are you doing here?" She felt awkward and at ease at the same time. Self-conscious and confident. He always had made her feel that way.

"I could ask you the same, baby girl." The smile he sent her way made her knees go weak and she gave herself a mental shakedown. When he crossed the floor and gave her a hug, she felt at ease. She wanted to stay in his arms for days just to feel safe again. Tears were prickling at the corner of her eyes, and she turned away so Janus and her dad wouldn't see them.

"There you are, Janus. Good, then my little girl is in safe hands. Make sure to get her out of that marriage with as little fuss as possible, you hear? Make it quick." Her dad turned to Emily and gave her a small hug. "I have an appointment at the mechanic, the old car has been making a fuss and your mother is worried something will happen if I drive in it." Rolling his eyes, he gave her another hug before walking toward the entrance. "Make sure to drop her off at home no later than 10 pm young man, or your father will hear from me."

"Yes sir." A smile spread across Janus' face again, but this time Emily didn't notice. "Shall we?" Janus swept out his arm, motioning toward an open door further ahead.

Shutting the door behind them, he sat down at his desk, pointing toward his guest chair on the other side.

"A divorce, huh?" Avoiding eye contact, Emily simply nodded. When she didn't provide him with any more information, he gave a small sigh and got up to find the papers to fill them out.

"You know if you just told me what happened, this would go faster. I don't fancy meeting in court just to be told a wild tale about something and not be able to have anything to fire back with. You know?" She still did not meet his eyes, which worried him. They'd been friends when they were children, sure they went separate ways when going to school, and the contact had been sparse, but still. It was his Ems, damn it. Getting up from his chair he walked around the desk and crouched next to her. "Ems?"

Her fingers were twisting and untwisting in her lap, a nervous habit she had since she was a child. One of his big hands covered both her smaller ones. This couldn't be good. Not good at all. When she finally lifted her face to look him in the eye, tears were spilling over and she gave him a weak smile.

"Sorry." She leaned over to grab the tissues on his desk Janus simply handed them to her.

"Nothing to apologize for." Reaching out and touching her arm, Janus noticed her winching. Narrowing his eyes, he didn't press further, but now he really wanted to know what the hell happened.

Last thing he heard was that she was pregnant and happy. Or that was what Sarah had told him.

"Wanna talk about it?"

"Not really, but you need to know what happened to get the divorce through." Looking at him with fear in her eyes, she lowered her voice. "Just don't tell daddy. He would freak if he knew how bad it was."

"What's the official story?" Emily got up from her chair and walked toward the window. There's a small garden out in the back, nothing fancy, but she couldn't help smiling when she saw the birdfeeder out there.

"Still feeding the birds during summer?" A chuckle came from Janus. "He cheated on me. Several times." The smile slid right off his face. Looking at her tense shoulders, he knew that the cheating wasn't the only thing.

"And unofficially?" He didn't like to push like this, but he needed to know. Stepping up behind her, he wrapped his arms around her, letting her know she's safe.

"He.. The cheating wasn't the worst." The last was said no higher than a whisper.

"I thought you were happy? The last I heard was that you were pregnant. What happened?"

"He… I don't know. I mean... I'm not sure what went wrong. Maybe the pressure of being the youngest partner in the firm got to him, maybe he got bored. I don't know." Turning around Emily looked up at Janus. "He started drinking more, and when he got drunk, he got mean. First it was just words, but -" Wrapping her arms around her body, a shiver went through her body.

"Did he hit you?" Ice ran through Janus' veins. The thought of someone hurting Ems chilled him to his core. When she nodded, anger rose. Stomping on it, he put on his professional mask.

"Do you have any proof? Any medical records, photographs..."

Without a word, Emily reached into her bag and pulled out a two inch thick file and handed it to him. "I might be naïve – or I was, but I'm not stupid. There are pictures, medical records, phone numbers for doctors who treated me, police reports. Hopefully it should be enough."

"I go through this later, but if everything is there, a divorce shouldn't take long. Now, what do you want from the divorce?"

"Nothing." Her answer surprised him a little. If he had been such an ass to her, why on earth wouldn't she flay him for everything? His surprise was noticed by Emily and she gave him a small smile. "I only want to be left alone. I don't need any money, I don't want any of the jewelry or clothes or any of the cars. I just want peace. The chance to start over again, far away from him. That's it."

Nodding his agreement, Janus wrote it down. "Got it. This definitely makes the divorce go through easier and faster as well. How much of this can I share with the judge?"

"Do what you feel you need to. Just make sure the divorce go through. I am done with him." Walking away from Janus, Emily picked up her bag and turned back toward Janus. "Let me know if you need anything else."

Before Janus could register what happened, Emily walked out of the door. Scrambling, he almost ran after her.

"Wait! Ems!" Turning around in the waiting area, Emily raised her eyebrows in surprise. "I promised your father I would make sure you got home."

A chuckle escaped her. "I'll be fine. I need to talk to my girls anyway, so don't worry. I can find my way home."

"Wait." Going back to the reception he grabbed a card and wrote down something on the back. "Here. In case you need something." Emily accepted it and looked down at it before tucking it into her jeans.

"Thank you, Janus. For everything." Watching her walk out of that door was the hardest thing he had to endure. The view of her ass swaying in those jeans was sweet, but he also knew she wouldn't jump into anything, not while the divorce was going on. Just the thought of her being beaten made him clench his hands in anger. Time to get to work.

***

Raising her hand to knock on that door was tough. Emily knew she had to do it, but damn. For the fifth time she lifted her hand to knock. For the fifth time she stopped right before she reached the door. With a quick tug the door is opened, and a woman stood on the other side, glaring at her.

145

"Are you ever gonna knock on that freaking door? Or are you gonna stand out here on the porch all day?" Sarah could be intimidating if she wanted to. Her small frame didn't stop her – at all. Although she wasn't so tiny right now with the baby bump protruding from her front. Her hair was as wild as it used to be, if she could, she would wear all the colors in the rainbow, and make it look good. Her green eyes looked Emily up and down before pulling her into a hug. "Come in doll. Tell me what happened."

Sarah ushered Emily into the kitchen, but before she even entered, a squeal came from the room and she was attacked by two more people.

"You're here, you're home!!"

"OMG, I can't believe you're finally back!!"

"Wait, what happened to your tummy? Weren't you pregnant?"

What felt like a hundred question was thrown at her at once, and even though she felt overwhelmed, Emily couldn't help but smile at her old friends. Sonya and Angela were fussing over her, shooing her over to the kitchen table, and before she knew it, there was a cup of tea in front of her and cookies on the table. They're all chatting around her about what had happened in the little town, apparently Janus coming back was the biggest news. It's a small town – any kinds of news are more than welcome.

"So, what happened hon?" Sonya took a sip of her cup of coffee, while peering at Emily over the rim of her cup. Her brown hair was pulled into a knot on her head, keeping it away from her face. Emily made a face. They needed to know and she would need their help and support to get through this shit, but she wasn't looking forward to telling them.

"What didn't happen?" A heavy sigh escaped Emily while she reached for the teapot to get a refill. "He." Em took a deep breath. "He cheated on me. With a secretary."

Gasps came from Sarah and Angela, Sonya was cursing the air blue.

"With the sister of one of his partners."

This time Angela cursed long and hard. Sonya and Sarah just stared at Emily.

"Another lawyer from a different firm – I even had the "pleasure" meeting her once. Oh…. I almost forgot. Our housemaid."

Sarah cursed, long and hard, followed by Sonya who would've had made sailors cover their ears. Angela got up, found the hard liquor and poured all of them a shot.

"We need this. Something tells me, you're just getting started." Emily looked at her glass, but didn't touch it.

"You're right. I'm only starting." Her long time friends looked expectantly at her, waiting for her to continue her tale. "The cheating was one thing. You're right Sonya, I was pregnant. I lost him."

"It was a boy?" Sarah absentmindedly stroked her own growing tummy.

"Yeah. Adam got home one night, he had begun to drink a lot, and no, I don't know why. Right now I don't care." Taking another sip from her teacup, Emily pondered on how to tell them. They wouldn't judge her, that she knew. They had all had each other's back since school. "That night he came home not only very drunk, but mean as well. I don't recall too much from that night, but. I know the end result; me at the hospital, broken ribs, swollen face, bruising all over my body and a miscarriage."

The silence was heavy in the little kitchen. Emily wrapped her arms around herself, trying to hold off the tears. The memory of waking up to the beeping machines and tubes hooked into her was awful enough. Adding the loss of her baby boy made it unbearable. Sarah was the first one to react. Getting up from her chair she walked over to Emily and wrapped her arms around her shoulder, giving her a hug.

"I'm so sorry doll. So damn sorry. Nobody should go through that alone. When did all this happen?"

"About a month ago. I had to wait for the cuts and bruises to heal enough that I could leave without being noticed too much. I went by daddy's lawyer today and filed for a divorce. Janus is handling it for me."

Angela was watching her carefully. She was always the most perceptive of them all.

"You haven't told your dad, have you?"

Shaking her head, Emily shivered at the thought. "I know how he will react. If Adam ever is stupid enough to come here to talk to me, daddy would murder him if he knew. I won't risk that. It's bad enough Janus knows."

"Uh-oh. I can't imagine Janus taking that lightly."

"He's just doing his job, Angela. Simple as that." Sonya snorted. When Emily looked over at her with raised eyebrows, Sonya pointed a finger at her.

"Nothing has never been simple between the two of you. We've all been waiting for you two to hook up since beginning of school." Leaning forward and crossing her arms over her chest, she raised one brow herself. "Once this fucking divorce gets through, do yourself and him a favor and give him a chance to prove to you what a good guy can do for you."

"I thought Adam was a good guy. Now?" Sighing, Emily got up from her chair to walk over to the sink. Looking out at the twilight, she felt that it fitted her. Standing in her own twilight right now emotionally, she was waiting for the morning to come so the sun could shine upon the destruction of her life so she could begin to pick up the pieces of her old life. "I left everything except a few clothes and some books that where mine before we met. "

"So you're not going back? No matter what?" Turning her back to the window, Emily looked over at Sarah.

"No. I'm not going back. I don't care how much he begs, or says he's going to change. I deserve something better than that. I'm not a doll that you can parade in front of your associates to put back on the shelf when you get home. I need someone who will respect me for who I am, and support me when I chase my dreams. I'm definitely not his personal punching bag either. I'm done." Looking over her shoulder, Emily sighed. "I'll better get going. Daddy set a curfew."

All three women walked over to Emily and gave her a joined group hug. For the first time in a long time, she truly felt home. Safe and cherished.

"Come on, I'll drive you home." Sonya nodded her head toward the front door.

"Thank you." Sarah grabbed a hold on Emily's sleeve before she walked out of the door.

"Don't be a stranger, you hear? If you need to talk, we're all here for you." Giving her a last hug, Emily snatched her bag and walked out of the door to Sonya's car.

***

On their way back to Emily's parent's house, Sonya and Emily talked about what happened. Being a small town, people would assume not much went on, but they were wrong. In a small community like this, everyone knew everything and even the smallest things got noticed. The rumors about Emily getting back into town was already flourishing, even more so when she was seen walking into the lawyer's office.

Stopping in the driveway, Emily's heart stopped. There was no mistaken the red sports car parked there. It wasn't the only car there though. A station car was parked next to it.

"Who's car is that?" Both said it at the same time. Sonya tilted her head.

"Is that Adam's car? I know the Volvo is Janus's car." Looking over at Sonya, fear settled into Emily's stomach twisting it into knots.

"This isn't good. I'll better get inside." Putting her car in park, Sonya got out of the car to, almost running after Emily.

"Hang on, I'm coming with you. Emily!" But Emily wasn't listening, running at full speed to her home, all she's hoping for was that something ugly wasn't waiting for her inside the house. Bursting through the front door, she practically ran into the living room with Sonya hot on her heels. Emily could hear that Sonya was on the phone with someone, but her attention was swiftly directed to the scene in her parents living room.

Her father was standing behind the chair her mother was sitting in, a stern look on his face. Her mother was twisting her hands, apparently they had the same nervous habit. Emily had forgotten all about that.

"Baby, there you are! I've been so worried about you!" Her head snapped toward Adam standing to the side, opposite her parents. Fear crawled up her spine. "Now that I found you, let's get back home. Say goodbye to your parents." Reaching forward, Adam tried to grab Emily's hand, but Janus stepped in between.

"She has filed for a divorce, the papers have been sent to your lawyer. She is not going with you." Crossing his arms over his chest, Janus suddenly seemed bigger, more menacing. Taking a step back, Emily backed straight into Sonya.

"Do you have any idea who I am?" Adam bellowed.

Inwardly Emily groaned. Raising one of his eyebrows Janus made a point of looking Adam up and down before answering.

"From the looks of it, you're a boy who never grew up and thinks that a woman is a play toy and not something to be treasured. You're also trespassing, so if you could just get out the same way you got in, everything should be fine."

"I'm not leaving without my wife. I don't care what legal measures you take, nothing will keep me away from her. She's mine." The last was barely a growl, and put Emily on the edge. She knew he wouldn't stop until he got what he wanted, or he completely understood that there was nothing to come for.

"I'm staying Adam. Nothing could persuade me to come back with you. I don't care what you promise." Swallowing her fear she sidestepped Janus and went nose to nose with her future ex-husband. "You hurt me. Badly."

Adam lifted his hand to touch her cheek. Not allowing it, Emily took a step back, bumping into Janus. Feeling him standing so close was amazing. Secure. Adam narrowed his eyes at the sight but didn't comment any further.

"I know I did, baby. I'm sorry, I would never be able to express how sad I am for what I did. It was a mistake and it won't happen again."

"You're right. It won't. Because I won't allow it to. Go back home Adam. I am where I belong – with my family and friends."

Clenching his hands, Adam narrowed his eyes in anger. When Janus gently laid his hand on Emily's arm, his patience ran dry.

"You don't belong to this shit place. I built you up, gave you everything you ever could need and want, and this is how you repay me? You ungrateful whore!"

"You gave me nothing but heartache and pain, Adam. Yes you bought shiny things, jewelry and new cars, but you was never there for me when I needed you, and always belittled me. You…" Emily stopped herself before she revealed how bad it really had been.

"You lost our son." Feeling herself going completely white, Emily closed her eyes for a few seconds to stem the pain she felt. He just delivered the ultimate low blow and the gloves came off. Opening her eyes, anger burned in them, making them go dark. She stepped right up in his face, hissing the words to him.

"No. Losing my son is not *my* fault, but *yours*." She felt Janus step closer to them both. "You pushed me down the fucking stairs, you kicked me repeatedly until I passed out – and then you kept going. I spent the better part of a month in the hospital because of you and your "treatment". You're an idiot if you think I'll ever fall for your sweet talk ever again." Stepping away from him, Emily pointed to the door. "Leave, Adam. You're not welcome here."

Adam moved so fast no one had the time to react. In seconds, he punched Emily in the face, grabbed her arm and was on his way to drag her out to the car, when he was tackled from behind by

Janus. Losing his grip on Emily, both men began to fight each other in the driveway. Sonya rushed over to Emily to make sure she was all right.

"The cops should be here any minute now," she quietly murmured to Emily, stroking her hair. As on request, the red and blue lights from a police car lightened up the darkness. Lying on the ground on her side, Emily could do nothing but watch helplessly when she saw the two officers step between the men and handcuff them both. A small "no" came from her when she saw Janus being dragged away, but she was too weak to get up.

"We'll get him out tomorrow, sweetheart. Don't you worry." Her mother's soothing voice was in her ear, and the last thing she remembered hearing is her father's voice. She was pretty sure he was cursing the air blue around him.

***

Waking up was a bitch, the light too bright in her room. Groaning, Emily tried to turn around in her bed, only to land with a thud on the floor. Laying there, she blinked a few times, trying to orient herself. Oh, right. Another groan made sure she got up on her feet, and after fighting the dizziness for a few seconds, she pulled on whatever clothes were closest to her, almost jumping on one leg while trying to get pants on and getting down the stairs.

"What's the rush, young lady?" Her father's voice made her stop up abruptly. Uh-oh. She knew that tone. Crap in a bucket, she was in so much trouble. Slowly turning to face her father, she wasn't all that surprised to see him standing in the doorway to the living

154

room, arms crossed over his chest and a good amount of anger radiating from him.

"I need to get Janus out of jail. He tried to help me yesterday, and he doesn't deserve to be there."

"We already paid the bail for him. You, on the other hand, have some serious explaining to do before you're leaving this house." Pointing to the kitchen, her father moved in there and Emily had no real choice but to follow. Sitting down at the kitchen table, her father poured himself a cup of coffee and made some tea for Emily. Once they're both situated at the table, Emily began to tell him everything that happened; from the harsh words, the drinking, to the beating that landed her at the hospital and losing her baby boy.

"As soon as I got released from the hospital, one of the male nurses drove me home, followed me inside so I could grab a few things and drove me to the rental car office. I drove straight here."

"You really meant what you said last night, didn't you? You're not going back to him, are you?"

"I would never go back to Adam. Ever. You taught me better than that daddy. I know I'm worth more than that. I'm not a punching bag and I'm not a doll to be put on a shelf only to be taken down when he needs to show me off. That's not who I am."

Satisfied with the answers his daughter gave to him, he leaned over to kiss her on the cheek.

"Now, let me drive you to town. I'm guessing you wish to check up on your young man."

"He's not mine daddy. He's a good friend, and I really want to thank him for what he did last night. I'm not sure what would've happened if Adam had gotten the chance to drive off with me."

"Lucky us, we don't have to find out. Now go get a shower and get some proper clothes on, I'll be waiting by the car when you're ready."

***

Getting out of the car, Emily noticed the police car holding outside Janus' office. Glancing back at her father, he simply waved at her before driving off. Stepping into the office, the receptionist glared at her before pushing a button on the intercom.

"Mr. Hansen, she's here." Glaring at Emily once again, the receptionist busied herself with paperwork. A door was opened further down the hall and she could hear Janus' voice.

"Come on in Ems." Without hesitation, Emily walked over to the open door and poked her head in. Suddenly Janus' office seemed much smaller compared to yesterday. Two police officers were standing in there, both looking up at her as she entered the room and closed the door after her. One of the officers stepped over to her, hand stretched out.

"Mrs. Hallberg, I presume?" Wincing at the mention of her married name, Emily took the officers hand and shook it.

"I would prefer it if you would call me Emily, or Miss Jensen, my maiden name. As I'm sure you already know, I have filed for a divorce." The officer nodded, he did know, he was just testing the waters.

"Well, Emily. Could you please tell us what happened yesterday?"

"Officer Larsen, is this really necessary? You've already got the statement from everyone else on the crime scene, do you need to burden my client with further pain?"

"It's all right Janus. I can handle it." So she told the officers what had happened and why she was filing for a divorce.

"I'm not supposed to tell you this ma'am, but we're still holding him. Apparently he's wanted in Copenhagen for fraud. They're sending someone down to pick him up."

"What?" The surprise knocked the wind out of her. Blinking Emily tried to make head and tales out of it, but draws empty. "What? How? Why?"

"We don't know miss. But it's safe to say he's going to jail for a long time. Now just to be sure in case he gets out before time, would you like to get a restraining order on him?"

Looking up at the officer from where she sat on the chair, Emily felt the world come back into focus. Blinking a few times, she heard the word restraining order, and suddenly it all made sense.

"I can get a restraining order?" Janus moved closer to Emily and crouched next to her. Touching her knee to make contact, he explained.

"Yes, you can. With everything that happened, and all the proof you have, coupled with the events yesterday I don't know one judge who wouldn't grant it to you. That said, he can still come to you, but he's not allowed and the police have to respond immediately if he does and someone calls it in."

"Then let's file for it. Can't hurt with the way he acted yesterday."

"I thought you might feel that way, so I took the liberty to fill out the paperwork, all you have to do is sign." Putting the paper down in front of her, Janus handed her a pen and after a quick read-through, Emily signed it.

"Now was there anything else you needed from us, officers? Otherwise I need to have a word with my client about her divorce."

Both officers assured them that they had all they needed and said their goodbyes. As the door closed behind them, Emily suddenly got nervous. Before she knew it, Janus was in front of her, crouching again.

"How are you feeling?" A small laughter escaped her before she looked up at his face and just as quick the smile vanished. With trembling fingers, Emily reached up to gingerly touch his swollen eye. When he winced a little, she retracted her hand immediately.

"Sorry, I didn't mean to."

Taking her hand in his, Janus gave her a smile.

"It looks worse than what it is. It will heal soon enough. Just a black eye." He guided her hand back to his cheek, but before releasing it, he turned his face against her palm and gave her a small kiss. Her pulse quickened at the sweetness, the tenderness in his gesture, and she could feel her walls crumble.

"I came because I wanted to thank you for what you did yesterday. I don't know what would've happened if." A shiver went through Emily's body at the mere thought of what her husband would have done.

"Hey, none of that Ems. We're all here now. We won't let anything happen to you." Cupping her face in his large hands, he gently stroked her cheeks with his thumbs. Looking into his eyes, Emily could feel how easily she could get lost in them. Frankly, if he smiled at her, she was lost. Had always been. Without warning, Janus leaned in and captured her lips in a kiss. It was a sweet gently kiss, a mere taste, and it left her craving more. When he nibbled at her bottom lip, she had to stop the moan that was close to escaping her. Opening her eyes when the kiss ended, Janus leaned his forehead against hers.

"Sorry, I shouldn't have. Not with everything that is happening to you -" Before he could protest anymore, Emily leaned in and kissed him right back. Wrapping her arms around his neck she leaned in further. Janus didn't need any further encouragement and pulled her down into his lap. Having her flush against him, awakened dormant feelings long buried. Licking her upper lip, and nibbling at her bottom one, gave him the award he was looking for; her moan. As soon as she opened her mouth, he slipped his tongue in, exploring her. One of his hands tangled in her curls at her neck, while the other started to explore the rest of her body. Finding his way under her shirt, he slipped his hand up her ribcage toward her breast, when a pained sound escaped her. Freezing in his tracks, he leaned back, not sure what just happened.

"Sorry, it's just…" Gently removing his hand from her ribcage, Emily pulled her shirt down. "It still hurts a bit." Furrowing his brow, Janus tried to raise the shirt to take a look, but when Emily pulled it down again, he looked up at her.

"I won't hurt you Ems. I just want to take a look. That's all." Shoulders sagging, she let her arms fall to the side, allowing him to lift the shirt and look. A small gasp escaped him when he saw the green and yellow bruising on her porcelain skin. Gently, he put his hand over some of the marks, noticing how they resembled a hand. Anger burned through his veins, and Janus cursed long and hard, making Emily jump.

"I'm sorry Ems, I didn't mean to frighten you." Removing his hand, he pulled her gently into a hug. "I just can't imagine why someone would hurt you. Ever. You're absolutely perfect, and to do this -" Shaking his head, Janus can't even finish the sentence. A weak smile played on Emily's lips.

"You have no idea how much that warms my heart." Leaning in, she gave him a short and sweet kiss on the lips. "Thank you. For everything."

"Come on, it's almost lunch time. Let me buy you something to eat."

"No really, you don't have to." Glaring at her while helping her up, Janus didn't take no for an answer.

"Ems, I swear, if you use the word fine, I'll drag you over the knee and spank you." She could tell it was a joke, but the image somehow got stuck with her and a slight blush crept up her cheeks. "Come on, let's grab some lunch before I decide that the only thing I want to have is dessert." The way his voice lowered at the last words, made her body shiver in a good way, her nipples hardened and a fire started in her core. Without a word, Emily turned around and almost ran from the office, Janus right behind her.

"The last she heard before the doors closed behind her, was Janus shouting over his shoulder at the receptionist that he'd going out for lunch. Taking a deep breath to calm her raging emotions, Emily closed her eyes and tilted her head up toward the sun, enjoying the warmth it spread.

A slight touch at her elbow brought her back to reality, Janus was smiling at her. "Ready to go?"

***

A few days later, Emily came back home after another day out in the city that was close to their hometown. With a sigh she let herself into her parents home. Kicking off her shoes, she fantasized about a hot shower and a warm meal. Her parents had taken a few days off from work and left for Germany so she had the house all to herself. She needed it. With everything she had planned and the life she was trying to build back up for herself, she needed some quiet. Trudging up the stairs, pulling off her clothes on the way, the bathroom beckoned her to get that promised shower. Before reaching her destination, there was a knock on the door.

Grumbling under her breath, Emily turned around and ran down the stairs. Ripping the door open, she growled at whomever was outside.

"You better have a freaking damn good excuse for interrupting." Her rant stopped short when she saw who was on the other side of the door. Twinkling dark blue eyes meet hers, and a smile to die for accompanied it. Drawing in a breath, Emily suddenly realized what she was wearing – or more accurately what she wasn't wearing. A blush crept up her cheeks. Janus' grin grew wider and his smile turned more mischievous.

"Well, this was a pleasant surprise. Had I known you would greet me dressed like that, I would've come by sooner." Emily felt like she was on fire, in a multitude of ways.

"I was on my way to the shower, I just came home from the city." Stepping inside, Janus leaned closer to Emily and gave her a kiss on the cheek. Holding up his hand, he showed what he brought with him. "Chinese! I'm so darn hungry, you have no idea!!" Laughter escaped Emily, her joy not containable. Janus smiled at her, enjoying to see her happy again.

"Thought you might be hungry. Why don't you jump into the shower and I'll get this sorted out?" Leaning closer, his lips brushed her ear, he lowered his voice to a whisper. "Unless you need someone to wash your back, of course."

Molten lava spread through her, and her swallowed hard. Having Janus so close and the image of them in the shower was almost too much for her. Almost. When she didn't respond, Janus made his move, and gently brushed his fingers against the tanktop she was wearing, dipped under it to touch the petal soft skin underneath. Drawing in a breath, Emily turned her head slightly toward him. Her intention was to say no, but looking into his eyes, seeing her own need reflected in his eyes, her determination wavered, and before she knew it, she could feel her back pressed against the wall, Janus' body against her front.

Dipping his head, he kissed her like a starving man, devouring her little by little, his hands roaming over her body.

"Janus." A moan escaped Emily, a plea from her lips, begging him for more. Dipping his head further, he nipped at her breast, easily finding the nipple. Sucking it into his mouth, he gently bit down through the tanktop, eliciting another moan from her. To his surprise, her hands that had been firmly holding onto his back, were now working on his belt and zipper. After a few seconds work, the charged silence in the hallway was broken by the sound of the zipper. When Janus felt Emily's hand slip down, he froze. Closing his eyes, he relished in her touch; her slender fingers wrapping around him, stroking him from base to crown, running her thumb over his sensitive head. Putting one hand against the wall by her head, he leaned his forehead against hers, their breath intermingling

Over and over, Emily kept stroking him, loving the feel of his silky skin between her fingers, the small bead of precome made her want to taste him, and she licked her lips in anticipation. One of Janus' hands had been clasping her hips, but was now moving toward her core. Stroking her pussy through her underwear, Emily

163

closed her eyes in pleasure. She could feel her release building and she longed to meet it. It had been far too long since she'd had good sex. Dipping under the silk, Janus pushed a finger inside of her, loving the feel of her wet folds. The combination of her squirming from his touch, her hand still stroking his cock and the moans that came from her was almost enough to send him over the edge. A kiss to his neck sent shivers down his spine, a groan of pleasure escaped him.

"I need you Janus. All of you." The meaning wasn't lost on him. Within seconds, he ripped the offending underwear away, lifted her up so she could wrap her legs around him, driving himself balls deep into her, making her shout his name in pure bliss. His lips found hers and while he drove into her over and over, he kissed her like she was the air he needed to survive.

The fire that burned inside of her was spiraling out of control and she let it. Feeling his cock drive into her, stretching her to the limit felt so, so good and before she knew it, his name left her lips as the orgasm spread through her body leaving her limp. Janus soon followed after, his own release making his dick twitch and his head spin.

"You feel so good, baby girl. I could do this all night, just to hear you scream my name." Nipping at her nipple, he drove himself into her once again, her moan music in his ears. Her breath was labored, sweat drenched her forehead, and the special glow to her cheeks... all of it made her even more beautiful to him.

164

"Wow." A chuckle escaped Janus. "I need that shower even more now." Pulling himself out of her, Janus took her face in both of his hands and gave her a kiss that made her toes curl. Nipping at her bottom lip, he refused to let her go just yet, needing her even more. The way she clenched his biceps with her hands, he knew she felt the same way.

"I'll fix the food, while you shower.

Emily quietly agreed and she began to walk up the stairs. Making the mistake of looking behind him to admire the view, Janus could feel himself grow hard again by the mere thought of water sliding over her beautiful skin. Her footsteps could be heard upstairs, and Janus looked down at the food sitting on the kitchen table. When he heard the shower come on, he left the food and without hesitation, he ran up the stairs, following the sound of water.

Janus quietly slipped into the bathroom, and for a minute he just stood there, enjoying her silhouette behind the drapes. Seeing her hands reaching for the soap and the way they traveled over her skin, Janus quickly shucked his clothes and moved toward the shower. Slipping in there, he smiled when seeing her surprised look.

"Thought you would need some help getting soaped up." Moving to stand behind her, he put soap on his hands and moved them over her skin. Leaning her head back against his shoulder a sigh escaped her.

"And you just thought you would volunteer?" Feeling his dick press against her ass, she pressed tighter against him, enticing him and fanning her own flames as well.

"Uh huh." His hands covered her breasts, rolling the nipples between his fingers. Feeling them go stiff, he chuckled a little. "You like that, don't you?" Pinching them a little harder, he felt his own cock grow even harder. "Put your hands against the wall." The order came without thought, his voice husky. Seeing her obey was a huge turn on for him, even more to see her sway her ass and looking over her shoulder with desire smoldering in her eyes.

Standing behind her, he kissed her shoulder, his hands covering hers. Slipping down further, Janus peppered her back with kisses as he let his hands glide down her arms, slowly, teasingly. Carefully he avoided the patches of skin that were still marred by healing bruises. Crouching behind her, he got the perfect view to her ass, and he nipped at her globes, the temptation too high. Sliding a finger inside her pussy, he pumped a few times, feeling how wet she was. Giving her a final nip on the ass, he stood up and slowly pushed his cock inside her aching folds. As he entered, a moan escaped Emily and she arched her back even more, allowing him to penetrate deeper. Janus leaned closer to Emily and licked her earlobe. Pressing herself against him harder, Emily tried to make him move. She needed him to. Want rushed through her veins, muddling her thoughts. Pulling out a little, he slowly pushed back inside again. For what felt like forever, he repeated the motion, driving Emily insane with need.

"Please Janus." She feel him pull out again, only to stop the motion.

"Please what, baby girl?" His voice was husky with repressed need, barely contained. When she tried to press backward he tightened his hold on her hips, halting her motion. "Say it." A whisper against her ear.

"Fuck me Janus. I need to feel you move inside of me. Please. I want you." A harsh breath released by her ear and right before he drove into her he whispered into her ear,

"I love it when you talk dirty. My own fallen angel." No more words were said as Janus picked up the speed and the only thing that could be heard at the moment was the running water and skin slapping against skin. "Almost there baby, are you with me?"

"Harder." Panting, Emily could feel the sweet ecstasy of release lying so close, just around the corner. A small sound of frustration escaped her, knowing what would happen next – he would secure his own release and leave her hanging in limbo, just like Adam always did. To her utter surprise and delight, Janus gripped her hip harder, pushing himself more roughly into her, driving her closer to the edge. With his other hand he stroked her clitoris, and in few seconds pushing her all the way, drawing a scream from her as her orgasm tore through her body. Pushing one last time into her, he shouted her name with his own release.

Leaning her cheek against the cold tile wall, Emily panted, trying to bring her heartbeat down.

"Baby girl, you're gonna be the death of me." A breathless laugh escaped Emily. She could barely stand on her legs, tears prickling at her eyes. Noticing her emotional state, Janus frowned.

"Are you alright? Did I hurt you?" Shaking her head, she couldn't form the words to explain. Instead she turned around and burrowed her head into his chest, trying to not let her raging emotions get out of control. Without a word, Janus wrapped his arms around her, giving her strength.

"I haven't felt so good for too long. I... He never..."

"Geez, are you telling me he couldn't even... Bastard." Leaning back, he tilted her head up. Looking into his eyes she falls into their depths, not ever wanting to leave. Love, understanding and desire smoldered in there making her feel not only loved, but safe as well. Leaning down to kiss her deeply, making her head swim, he pulled her flush against him. "I would never leave you hanging baby girl. Ever. Come on. Let's get dried, dressed and get some dinner. I don't know about you, but I need some food to keep up with you." A chuckle escaped Emily as she untangled herself from him and she walked past him toward her room. Before leaving the bathroom, Janus delivered a saucy grin accompanied by a smack on her ass.

"Smart ass."

"Yeah. But admit it, you like my ass." Wiggling her ass, Emily giggled as she continued back to her room.

***

Two months later:

Opening the last box, Emily could hear the phone ring in the background.

168

"Karen?" No response. "Damn it, where she's at now?" Grumbling under her breath, she rushed toward the front room, hurtling toward the phone, grabbing it in the last second.

"I'm at the hospital, hubby is with me. Can you get Nugget and come?" Relief ran through Emily, followed by happiness.

"Of course Sarah. Don't you worry. Do you want me to come to the hospital, or keep him here?"

"Could you take him to the hospital? I don't want him to see me in pain, but I want him to see his sibling."

"You got it. On my way."

***

Arriving at the hospital, Emily was happy to see both Angela and Sonya there, waiting as well. Giving Nugget some crayons and a coloring book, they all four sat down to wait.

After a few hours, Sarah's husband poked his head out to wave them in, smiling at his son. Everyone tiptoed into the room, curious to see the newest member of the little family.

"Hey. Are you alright?" Emily looked at Sarah, who gave her a tired smile.

"Yeah, we're fine. Come and meet your little sister, sweetheart." Hugs and kisses were given and after a few minutes, the three friends left the little happy family. Hooking arms together they walked outside the hospital toward their cars.

"Have you heard from Janus yet?" Angela looked over at Emily, who shook her head.

"No." Sorrow stabbed her in the heart. Trying to push it away, she gave both Sonya and Angela a smile. "I'm sure he's just busy. He'll call when he has the time." Even when she said it, she knew it was a lie. It hurt that he wasn't there, more than she thought it would. Brushing it away, she gave her friends a last hug before getting into the car.

Arriving at her apartment, she could see lights burning in the store. Sighing under her breath, she got out of her car.

"Damn it Karen, all I asked was that you shut of the lights and locked the doors." Sighing again, she walked up to the front door of the store, only to find it unlocked. Furrowing her brow, she opened the door and walked inside. Looking around, nothing looks out of place. Noticing a forgotten coffee cup on the table, Emily grabbed it on her way to the back.

Pushing open the back door, she stopped right in her tracks, gasping. The entire back room had been changed; a blanket lying on the floor, a small picnic set up, candles burning all over the room. Blinking her eyes to make sure she wasn't dreaming, a shadow moved from the darkness.

"Do you like it?" Unable to respond coherently, Emily simply nodded.

"It's.... I... You did this? For me?" Tears were gathering in the corners of her eyes and Emily blinked rapidly a few times to clear her sight. Stepping up to her, Janus took her face in his hands, removing a single tear with his thumb.

"For you." Giving her a gentle kiss, he stepped back afterwards to look at her. "I'm sorry I wasn't there at the hospital. I just got home. I have something for you that you might like though. As compensation for being away all week." Ice spread in her blood, making goose bumps appear on her arms. She was getting better at not comparing Janus to her past experience with Adam, although sometimes little things brought it up, just like now. Adam had always bought her some trinket when he had been doing something behind her back. Realizing she was still standing with the coffee cup, she moved toward the kitchen area to put it down.

"Ems?" Hearing him call after her didn't help. Putting the cup down, she grabbed the counter to steady herself. "I got these while I was at a boring meeting." Leaning over her shoulder, he placed a kiss on her bare shoulder before laying down a folder before her. Surprise removed the ice enough for her to reach out with trembling fingers to open it.

Inside was her freedom. Literally.

Turning toward Janus, she opened her mouth, but no words came out. Instead she leaned her forehead against his chest, heaving her breath in and out. Her shoulders shook, she released all the pent up fear and anger she had held too close to her heart for far too long.

"I thought this was worth celebrating."

Laughter escaped Emily and she nodded.

"You're right. " Touching the papers with a fingertip, Emily smiled. "I can't believe the divorce finally went through." Wrapping her arms around his neck to bring him closer to her, she gave him a devious smile. "Now…. What kind of celebration did you have in mind?"

"The very naughty kind baby girl. The best kind."

THE END

CONTROL

By Caroline Baker

I said...

Baby, I feel scared

I've never had

My hands not there

And I'm sitting here

Totally exposed

Without any

Of my clothes

And it's so hard

For me to try

And even look you

In the eye

He said...

Baby, Hush

I'm right here

And there is nothing

For you to fear

I know that this
Isn't easy
But you're trying
Just to please me

He leaned in
And kissed my lips
Placed his hands
On my hips

Pulled me close
Deepened the kiss
I feel my body
Respond to this

He takes his finger
And with the lightest touch
Circles my nipple
Making me blush

When it puckers
And pulls up tight
I feel my pussy
Clench and I fight

Not to cum
Then and there
When I feel his fist
Clench in my hair

Deepens it more
Pulls me in
Pinches my nipple
And I begin

To move my hips
Round and round
But no friction
Can be found

I start to whimper
As my need builds
I want so badly
To be filled

Start to struggle
Against the rope
To free my hands
Is my only hope

He says...
Baby, don't fight
I know what
You need tonight

He pulls back
I feel dazed
He tips my chin up
To catch my gaze

Desire is burning
In his eyes
He says lean back
And I comply

Takes the flogger
Starts in on my tits
It stings so good
Each time it hits

He catches my nipple
And I cry out
My pussy is dripping
And I have no doubt

That he can smell
My desperation
And feel my growing
Frustration

I start rubbing
Against his jeans
Hoping for friction
From the seams

He keeps hitting
And I feel the burn
And my mind
Starts to turn

I start to give in
Just let it flow
Let him take
Over control

I'm lost in the moment
The pleasure and pain
When I feel
His hand move in

He undoes his jeans
Pushes them down
His cock springs free
Bead glistening on the crown

My mouth suddenly
Begins to water
And my need rises
As I get hotter

My pussy weeps
Crying to filled
To be the place
His seed is spilled

Flogger still moving
In his left hand
He drops it now
So he can stand

Lifts me up
Then slams me down
On his cock
And turns around

Backs up fast
I hit the wall
He starts moving
Giving me all

Of his power
His hard upward thrust
Pounding my cunt
Until I just

Can't take anymore
And I let go
Drenching his cock
As my juices flow

I keep cumming
Just can't stop
Screaming his name
As he goes over the top

In and out
He glides real slow
Looks in my eyes
And I know

I give him this power

When I feed his need

To dominate me

So we both are freed

He kisses me softly

I slide down slow

He says

I love you, Baby. Hope you know.

INEVITABLY YOU

By Aurelia Fray

ZERO.

~Izzy~

"Izzy, baby, look at me," Trey begged me. The floor, which had captured my anxious gaze, swam in and out of focus.

"I…can't…I can't," I stuttered through salty tears. The whirls in the ancient wooden floorboards were moving now, sliding around and reordering themselves into unfamiliar patterns.

"You can. I need you to look at me. This isn't what it looks like," he pleaded. His words stabbed me. I wished they could cut out what I had just seen—what I had walked in on—but nothing would remove that from my memory. The woman on her knees in front of him made a strangled, gargling sound, but her mouth was full so she wasn't intelligible.

"Just wait, Zara. I will let you up in a moment," he snapped and ironically, I felt sorry for her. His sharpness demonstrated a startling lack of concern for the semi-naked woman. Was it really only a moment ago that he stared at her with passion in his eyes?

"Izzy, you need to look at me and focus on what I am saying, okay Baby?" he whispered gently trying to micro-manage my reaction to this *clusterfuck*. When I hesitated, he roared. "Now!"

My eyes flicked upward. Despite the harsh order, I witnessed his soft and patient gaze focused upon me. "That's good, Angel. Now, I need you to understand what is going on. Look around the room and take in the scene, Izzy. See what I *am* and *am not* doing." He put much more emphasis on what he wasn't doing, so I tried to focus on that instead. However, he was a clever bastard because it transpired that I couldn't do one without the other.

"Out loud, Baby."

"Your bed is a mess. There are things all over it." I stumbled to release the words from my mouth. I tried to find the most innocuous thing in the room to look at. Yet, even there, on the rumpled sheets, were things I didn't want to see. Oils, silk ribbons, a chain attached to a metal bar, something that looked like my hairbrush but without the bristles.

"What else?"

"You, you're wearing only your leather pants and you . . . you have a whip in your hand."

"Not a whip. This is called a—"

"I don't care what it is called!" I bawled frantically. The shock was wearing off. I was freaking out. How could he be so rational?

"Okay, Izzy, what else?" I couldn't quite believe he wanted me to continue detailing the scene, but I knew if I didn't, he wouldn't let it go. He would keep me here until I saw what he wanted me to see.

"What else? *What fucking else?*" I screamed, "You have a semi-naked woman, bound by her wrists and ankles, kneeling in front of you with a ball gag in her mouth. You two-timing, no-good, fucked-up, lying piece of shit!" Finally released from my haze, I let loose my more immediate anger.

"But, Izzy, look. It's not sex. I'm not technically cheating. I don't want you thinking I betrayed you in that way, Baby."

"This? This is not a betrayal? This isn't cheating? Are you damaged in the head? Did you hit yourself with that thing? Of course this is cheating. *You have another woman in your bedroom*! Are you trying to say this wouldn't have progressed to fucking?"

The woman moaned behind the large black ball in her mouth and Trey bent down to release her from her bindings. He did it slowly, taking care to caress each limb before he released the next buckle. When he proceeded to reach for a tube of gel and lather her in it, I left the room.

I should have walked out the second I caught him slapping at her flesh with that fringed stick-thing, but the woman's pleasured moans and Trey's blissed-out expression had stunned me into becoming an unwilling observer. It took nearly three minutes for him to spot me in the doorway. Those three minutes felt like an eternity.

I packed a bag with random items of clothing. I needed to leave. I knew my best friend Kye would take me in for a while; he was the best option I had. For once, I was glad Trey and I had maintained separate rooms. I wouldn't have coped if I had to stay in there for a moment longer. The humiliation of packing my things in front of his other woman would have killed me.

For the last three months, Trey slept with me in my room. Before that, we were simply colleagues that shared an apartment. I'd found it odd that we only ever stayed in my bed, that Trey kept his room locked, but now his reticence made sense. Well, a fucked up kind of sense, anyway.

He edged into my room fifteen minutes after I'd left his. He stayed silent at first but when we heard the door close behind Zara, he began to speak.

"I understand why you are upset, Izzy—"

"Good for you!"

"But it isn't a sexual thing. Well it *is* kind of, but we don't have sex. Zara and I, we have a mutual need."

"Shut up. I really don't want to hear it."

"You need to know. You have to understand. I love you. You are mine. I make love to you and no one else, Baby. Zara and me—"

"Zara and me. *Zara and me*! For fuck sake! Why do you care whether I understand this? *Zara and you* can go fuck yourselves!" I spat the words into his face.

"Zara and I," he continued, undaunted by my anger, "we like to give and receive. We indulge in a little bit of danger play; exploring pleasure and pain. Nothing too heavy, nothing too dark, just light spanking and flogging. A little bit of command and control. Do you understand what I am telling you?"

"You like to beat her; she enjoys getting beaten. I get it." I slammed my shoes into my case and threw my makeup bag on top of the pile.

"What are you doing?"

"Leaving. You lied to me. Maybe not openly, but by omission. You should have told me. I would never have got involved—" I didn't mean the words in the way they came out but it was too late to take them back. Trey looked devastated. He looked how I felt.

"If that's what you want."

"No that's not what I *want,* Trey! I am destroyed. I fucking love you. I thought you felt the same. I gave you my trust and you were playing with me the whole time. I'm the girl you fuck nightly and she is the girl who really gets your rocks off."

"I wanted to tell you. I would have given her up if I thought you would be interested in—"

"In what? Letting you tie me up and beat the crap out of me?"

"That's not how it works!" He shouted in return. My ignorance annoyed him but he never gave explaining a chance and it was too late. The damage was done.

I pulled my bag onto my shoulder and faced him. I felt determined. I had to be strong.

"I want you gone before I get back." I said these last words before I walked out the door. My heart kept it together until I got to Kye's place and then it burst into a hundred million jagged pieces.

185

ONE.

Trey Grant ruined me.

It had been three years since the last day I saw him and that statement was as true now as it was then.

Trey Grant ruined me.

Those words rebounded around my head as I reclined on a luxurious bed, in a five-star hotel, in the middle of Paris. The man above me—*Pierre? Emillion? Jean-luc? Who knows?*—grasped for the hooks of my bra and I was not making it easy for him. Why? Because I already knew the outcome: He would grab, pinch, poke, smother me in his spit and utter nonsensical grunts into my hair as he thrust himself, messily, into my body. Then, after all that, I would still have to fake an orgasm, make a weak excuse and kick him out of my hotel room so I didn't have to wake up next to a stranger. That was the inevitable ending to my night.

I had hoped the romantic setting and the excitement of a one-night fling with a handsome stranger would heat a fire in my knickers, but no—nothing. The only outcome of a moderately pleasurable date was a horrible choice: indulge in meaningless sex with my handsome French tour guide or send him packing with his dick half-mast and a frown on his chiselled face.

What to do?

"Isabella? Where did you go, my sweet?" *What'shisname* whispers at the side of my neck. In a cheesy novel, the writer might have said his words caressed my ear, but this wasn't romance. I was on used bed linen and his words tickled. The only desire I felt was the desire to put a finger in my ear hole and wiggle it about. I was not in the mood.

"I think we should stop. This is a mistake." I sighed. His eyes narrowed. The annoyance in his gaze was piercing but I wasn't going to back down. He stared down at me for a few tense seconds, then sat up, buttoned his shirt and moved to the edge of the bed.

"This is you, yes?" he murmured scornfully, his accent becoming stronger.

"Pardon me?"

"It is not me. It is you with this problem?" His anger made his English sound harsh and broken but I understood him. He was looking for some kind of assurance that he was still sexy and manly. It was never my intention to insult him, so I told him what he wanted to hear.

"Jean-Claude—"

"Philippe!" he snapped. *Oops shit.*

"I know who *you* are." I thought fast. "Jean-Claude is my boyfriend back home. He would be really disappointed in me. I should not have gone to dinner with you tonight, but you tempted me. Only now, now I feel conflicted but I can't betray my boyfriend's trust." I wailed, clutching a hand to my heart and forcing tears into my eyes. I had no idea if he understood me, or if he

187

believed my blatantly over-performed lies, but the tension flowed from his body. His shoulders slumped in acceptance of defeat and he grudgingly nodded.

"You are a beautiful woman, Isabella." He leaned over me and kissed my forehead. The small gesture startled me and I had to swallow back a self-pitying sob.

"Merci, Phillipe."

He walked to the door. As his large hand reached for the ornate handle, I felt a stab of regret. *Was I making a mistake? Should I just see it through?* I needed someone to obliterate Trey from my memory. It had been so long since I took a lover, I was starving for the touch of a man, although not hungry enough it seemed, when I couldn't bring myself to ask Phillipe to stay. At the last second, Phillipe grabbed his thick cock through his trousers and squeezed.

"I would have fucked you into next week!" He postured then closed the door on his retreating figure. His words hung in the air.

"You would have tried," I mumbled aloud to dispel them. Truth was nobody else but Trey would do. I might have thrown him out but we never had a chance to sort it all out. He didn't stick around to fight for me. He never stayed long enough to know I would have forgiven him. That I still wanted him. I groaned aloud into the silent hotel room. In the end, it was always just me alone in a room with a skilled hand and my twisted memories of Trey.

TWO.

"How was the trip?" I heard him before I could see him. My best friend shouted to me as I pushed my baggage trolley through the labyrinth of pathways at the airport.

"Sucked monkey balls!"

"Shit, honey, you mean you didn't get laid?" He bellowed so loudly that the two old women in the line behind me huffed with disgust. I shook my head and grinned at the jerk. He had a habit of embarrassing me. He said his harassment was character building but really he was just a dickhead.

"Kyle Francis Zabuto! You wash that filthy mouth!" I laughed. He shot me a withering look upon hearing his full name made public and then returned the favour. I was almost out of the man-made maze but I dashed to clamp a hot sweaty hand over his mouth before he could do any real damage. I didn't make it in time.

"Isabella Jane Harrison, if you don't let some poor bastard plunder that lady-cave of yours, it is going to seal itself back up! Or worse. It will grow teeth and eat alive the next poor fool that ventures too close!"

"Shut the hell up!" I groaned, slapping him across the back of the head. "What are you doing here anyway? I thought Samantha was coming to get me?"

"She bailed."

"So I see."

"She had to - there was something she had to do."

"Sounds vague. Important I assume?"

"Very." That abrupt explanation was all I was going to get on Samantha's absence. I assumed she asked him not to tell me and, although I was curious, I knew that if I needed to hear the details they would share them.

"Okay. Take me home, Kye."

"Yeah, um, about that—"

"What? What now, Kye?"

"Sam has people staying at your apartment."

"What the fuck? She can't do that. What the hell is she thinking?"

"It's complicated, Izzy. There is an act booked at the club for a week and Sam needed to house them."

"So rent them a goddamn room at a hotel, don't give them my fucking bed for the week! She might be my landlord, and yeah I live over her club, but this is ridiculous. My stuff? My bed? My privacy? A stranger invading my personal space? Nuh uh! Take me home. Right now! I mean it, Kye."

"Shit. Calm the fuck down, Izzy. They won't be in your room. They won't go near your stuff. I promise."

"You promise? *You* are giving me a personal guarantee, Kye? What's going on? Plus, the only other room is Trey's and no one gets in there. He locked it before he left and still pays his half of the rent, so Sam can't have given them that."

The idea of someone else in Trey's room was almost worse than someone in mine. It carried with it a finality that I did not want to face. Of course, I doubted he would come back. I knew I wouldn't wake up to him cooking bacon and eggs in the kitchen or smell his thick tar coffee ever again, but I lived in hope. This news was dashing the last shreds of that hope to pieces.

Kye shot me furtive glances from the side of his eyes. I hated him right now. Hated that he knew more than me and wasn't sharing, hated that Sam and he seemed to be in cahoots and against me, but mostly, I hated that he thought I needed to be handled with care like some piece of ornate glass. I broke a long time ago. What I had managed to piece back together, over the years, was stronger; no longer as pretty, but not as delicate either.

"You were never meant to find out about it. You shouldn't have finished your trip so soon," Kye grumbled lifting my bags from the trolley and hulking them to his car. I wasn't sure how he managed it without getting towed, but he was parked in a no stopping zone. His engine idled throatily.

"Sorry to have ruined your secret plans." I sulked and I didn't care. The ride back to town was uncomfortable and filled with a thick tension. Kye tried a few times to break the silence by asking me questions about my vacation, but I ignored him and stared out of the window instead of answering. By the time he pulled up outside the club, he was furious with me.

"Just so you know, we did this for you. Your choice to return early was a fucking nightmare scenario and Sam and I had a complete meltdown trying to find the best solution to the problem. Staying a week at mine was the best option for *you*, but instead of just going with it, you had to argue. Well go on then. Go in and see what your lack of trust gets you," he yelled. Kye flung open his door, stormed to the back and pulled my bags from the trunk. He dumped them on the paving and then yanked open my door. I was too stunned to move. Never before had Kye yelled at me and I was torn between crying and kicking his ass for being so bloody indignant. I was the one being wronged. Wasn't I?

"Get out!" he snapped. As soon as I closed my passenger door, he circled around the back, got in and sped off, leaving a puff of exhaust fumes and black skid marks on the road.

Shocked, numb, confused, and tired, I dragged my stuff up the stairs and into my apartment.

THREE.

I kicked the door shut behind me. Firstly, in protest to my not-so-happy homecoming and secondly, to warn my unwelcome house-sitters that I was in the building. I stood still for a few beats, watching for signs of life, but no one hurtled out of my room, nobody stumbled from the bathroom or Trey's room. In fact, looking around, there seemed to be no change to my apartment whatsoever. Everything remained exactly as I'd left it.

I scanned the kitchen sink for dishes. Not even a teaspoon cluttered the basin. *Perhaps Sam changed her mind? Perhaps, when she heard I was coming, home she evicted them? But then, why would she send Kye for me and why would she tell him to take me back to his place?* Nothing made sense.

I dragged my luggage to my room and kicked it into the corner. I would deal with unpacking later. First thing first, I need to make sure everything was in its place. I did the rounds, trying to recall every detail and surprisingly realised that I took my home for granted. Everything seemed okay but, then again, nothing was certain. Had I really left the black vase on the back table or was it usually on the windowsill? Did I have a habit of leaving the remotes on the chair or was I careful about putting them back on the centre table? I didn't bloody know.

In the bathroom, I found it— the first clue that someone else had been here—a yellow striped toothbrush stood in my glass. I picked it up and spun it around in my hand. The bristles were well-worn and still wet. Below it lay my toothpaste, rolled up neatly. Another confirmation. I was a squeezer not a roller.

"Fuck! I am going to fucking kill you Sam!" I screamed out, feeling the words tear at my throat. My voice seemed to fill up every inch of the apartment. I reached into my purse, discarded earlier by the front door, and grabbed my phone. Dialling Sam's number was habit, my fingers trained. It rang and rang. "Answer damn you!"

"Don't start with me!" She barked as soon as she connected the call.

"You have got some fucking explaining to do, Bitch."

"Kye called already. It's more complicated than he told you. Look I can't talk right now." Music blared in the background. The telltale screech and whine of an amplifier indicated she was downstairs in the club.

"I'm coming down; you can tell me in a minute."

"Don't you dare! I'm working. I can't drop everything for you. Just wait up there. I will be up in half an hour."

"No. I'm not waiting. Now Sam! You owe me an explanation." I heard her hiss out a long breath. Her footsteps clip-clopped across the floor, the music increased in volume. She stopped, told me to *"hang the fuck on"* before I overheard her speaking with someone else.

"She is back and I'm going to have to tell her." There was a masculine sigh and a voice, familiar to me, rumbled, "I understand."

Two words and tears welled-up in my eyes. Two words and my whole body went into nervous spasms. I shook like a leaf and a lump swelled in my throat, making it hard to swallow. I stood there like that, quivering and trying to swallow saliva over that blasted lump, for I don't know how long. It was long enough for Sam to finish-up downstairs and walk into the apartment. When she looked at me, the colour drained from her face.

"Fuck fuck fuck! I am so sorry, Angel."

"Don't...call me...that." I stuttered on barely-there-breath.

"I didn't want you to know. He is only here for a few days and is scheduled to headline at the club on the Barhoopla tour. I am so sorry, Babe."

"I...I...is he...is he downstairs right now?"

"Yeah, they are doing a sound check. I said he could use the closed bar for rehearsals." Sam hovered, watching me in silence. I could tell that she was analysing my reactions and that I was only one crazy outburst away from being shipped to my mother's house in a straitjacket.

"I understand." I heard the words, a lesser rendition of Trey's, leave my lips. Sam accepted them as an admission of defeat and I suppose they were, only not in the way she thought.

"Come on, Izzy, let's get you packed. You can stay with me until Kye gets over himself."

"No." Sam's eyes bulged at my response. My shaking had lessened. I straightened my spine and held my head up. "I am not leaving. This is my apartment. It has been mine for three years."

"He still pays half the rent. You want me to tell him he can't stay in his own room?" She groaned, flinging her arms into the air at my suggestion.

"No. That's not what I mean. I am trying to say that I won't run and hide just because Trey Grant is back in town. I am not a coward. I can handle a few days."

"What if *he* doesn't want that?"

"Then *he* should have booked a hotel."

Sam grimaced but knew I was right. Trey didn't plan the Barpalooza tour. He had no idea I was going on vacation. It said a lot that he returned to the apartment under the assumption that I was still here. I reasoned it all out in my head and, as I did, I felt stronger. I wanted to see him. It was time to put this thing to bed.

"Look, I don't think that is a good idea. You two didn't exactly part on friendly terms."

"We didn't part on any terms. I kicked him out and he took off. It has been a long time since that day. I can handle it." Sam shook her head. She didn't trust me at my word and I couldn't blame her, she helped to pick up the pieces after Trey left. She knew what it did to me.

"You were a shivering mess not two minutes ago."

"Shock. I'm over it."

"I need to speak to Trey."

"No. You don't." His voice resounded as he pushed open the unlocked door and stood behind Sam.

I hoped seeing him again would humanise him in my mind. Over the years, I placed him on some mind-fucked pedestal, elevating him to a God-like status. He was the love of my life, the one that got away, the one that broke my heart. I secretly wanted my ideal image of Trey dashed by the reality of the man that stood before me.

Not so.

Trey Grant was *more* than I remembered. He was taller and broader. His tattoos were darker and the scruff on his chin was wilder than I credited him with. In the second it took for my eyes to drink him in, I realised that the man who walked away from me had been nothing more than a grown boy. The Trey that stood in front of me now was pure man. Pure unadulterated man.

"Sam, it is fine. Isabella and I have some catching up to do."

"I don't think this is a good idea." She tried, in a vain last-ditched attempt, to prevent the inevitable meltdown.

"And I'm telling you, it is fine," he insisted, his voice ringing with command. Sam glanced back and forth between us. Her eyes begged me to make a decision—the right decision.

"Trey is right. It will be fine. Three years is a long time. Go. I will call you later."

"But you—"

"Samantha, Isabella can make up her own mind. If she needs you, I am sure she will do as promised and call you. Oh, before I forget, the boys need more cables." His self-assured attitude and cool voice oozed control. Samantha cowered, taking a retreating step toward the door. He intimidated me too and that was a problem, a big fucking problem, because ever since the night I watched him with Zara, the thought of Trey Grant commanding me made my insides burn.

Being alone with Trey was either going to be the best decision I had ever made or the worst.

FOUR.

~Trey~

Isabella, stood before me with her hands on her hips, an adorable pout on her lips and hate in her eyes. She was trying to exude indifference but I felt the tension in her body from where I stood. It poured out of her like molten energy and yanked the hairs on my skin to attention. She was still the most beautiful thing I ever laid eyes on. She ordered me gone three years ago, and yet, I still felt exactly the same about her. I knew, even then, I was in love with her and time hadn't changed that for me.

However, I disgusted her and, from the way she looked at me with such pain, I could see time hadn't changed that for her.

"Izzy." I nodded in greeting, turning to lean my guitar case against the wall. I should have stayed in the bar, but the temptation to see Izzy was too much for me. I ditched the rest of the band, mid-rehearsal, and made my way to the apartment we once shared. Seeing her was like taking a knife to the gut and receiving redemption all at once.

"Trey," she responded, her voice tight. This was difficult for her. I understood.

"You look well." It was an understatement. She looked stunning. The skinny little thing from a few years ago had blossomed into a shapely, gorgeous woman. I tried not to stare yet I wanted to drink her in. Three years without her left me thirsting.

"Thanks. You too."

This stilted conversation was killing me but I shouldn't have expected anything more. "Coffee?" I asked and glided toward the kitchen counter. My machine sat in the corner where it had always been and I wondered if it meant something that she hadn't put it away.

"Sure, but not black like you always make it." She chuckled. The sound stifled as she stopped her laughter mid-way.

"I know. Creamer." I didn't turn around to face her. I knew she would be pissed with herself for slipping into her casual ways, even if we were only discussing coffee.

"So, where do we start?" I keep my tone bright, trying desperately to spur something close to a normal conversation.

"Are you asking me?"

"Sure. Tell me what you have been doing. How is your life?" I asked. Her potential response made me sick with anxiety. She could tell me that she was great, that her life was perfect and she was seeing someone who made her happy. If that was the case, I had to be happy for her. She would never be able to accept my lifestyle and I couldn't ask her to.

Izzy sank into the sofa. The motion wasn't one of a person seeking comfort or familiarity. There was no casual air to it. She slumped. She looked broken and tired and I knew we were going to say all the things that went unsaid the night we split.

"Why didn't you tell me before?" she whispered. She remained quiet but hardy. She showed bravery.

"I didn't think you would accept that part of me. I didn't know how to tell you without you thinking I was strange or dangerous," I explained, unaware of the inherent condemnation.

"I wasn't given the chance to understand," she defended.

"When I asked you to give me a chance, you ran away," I accused in response, but regretted my harsh tone as soon as the words were off my tongue.

"I don't want to argue."

"I agree. It is okay that you don't like my lifestyle. I get it. It isn't the easiest thing to understand or accept and it is probably best that we found out when we did." I tried to placate her. I wanted her to know that I understood her viewpoint.

"You think it was your kinky tastes that upset me?"

"Well, yeah."

"Jeeze, Trey. Have you seriously not understood your betrayal these three years?" Her voice carried around the room. Relief flooded me. To see her so passionate, even if it was bottled-up anger, gave me hope. Anger was better than apathy.

"I did. I do. But I don't think you fully understood the scenario."

"Ok. Let me explain. You told me you loved me. We shared everything about our lives, or so I thought. You moved into my room. We had a fucking fantastic sex life and then I came home to see you playing with another woman. One that you obviously had an intimate relationship with, sex or not," she added as I motioned to argue. "You engaged in activities that I had no idea you were interested in, and did so in a space that you never once invited me into. You were living two lives."

She was totally right. She had only stated the facts, and yet, for the first time, I saw her perspective clearly. I was a complete ass.

"Do you need me to explain how that made me feel?" she continued on a roll.

"I can guess." I mumbled, embarrassed to have been so wrong all this time.

"I would rather you knew. I was devastated. You didn't think it was worth telling me. You obviously didn't find me enough of a woman to fulfil your needs. You allowed another woman into *our* home and shared your secrets with *her* instead of me." She glared at me but her bubbling blue eyes betrayed the hurt beneath the anger. She blinked the welling tears away furiously.

"I am so sorry, Izzy. I am so so sorry. I thought you were disgusted with me. I thought I lost you because of who I was, not what I had done."

"No. I was in shock. Seeing you with her. You should have just told me."

"I didn't know if you would be receptive. I met Zara," Izzy flinched at the name, "at a club two years before I met you. We both understood that it wasn't anything more than an occasional thing. She was married, but her husband didn't enjoy bondage or rough play. Zara needed it in the same way that I needed to—"

"Control? Dominate?" Izzy finished for me. She sat forward in her seat watching me. Something had shifted in her expression. She was interested. She was intrigued and completely turned on by the idea. I read it all over her. Her tells hadn't changed in the three years we'd been apart. She clenched her legs together, squeezing her pussy tight to feel the pulse at her clit. Her eyes widened. Her tongue wet her lips before her bottom teeth nibbled upon her upper lip. One hand remained squashed between her tight thighs as the other gripped the sofa arm.

"I had no idea—"

"What?" her glare narrowed.

"That you would be so," I stalked towards her, drawn to her desire in a way that made me weak. She had no idea but she *owned me* and I fucking wanted her. "receptive," I finished, kneeling down in front of her so my legs encompassed hers.

"What makes you think I'm receptive? You assume too much, Trey!"

"Isabella, don't bullshit me, baby. I can read you. You are written upon my heart. You are a part of me and I will always know you." She pulled back in an unconscious attempt to protect herself. By creating space between us she was trying hide who she was, what she wanted, but she only revealed more to me. Layers and layers of hurt and distrust had entrenched her within the shell she had erected but, beneath it all, she was still my Izzy. I needed to prove she could trust me.

"It's been a long time, Trey. I am not that little lovesick girl anymore."

"So I see, but Izzy—" I leaned in and brushed my lips across hers whilst I breathed in her skin. I had missed her scent. Fruity and sweet.

"Hmm?" She hummed against my mouth. The heat of her flesh beneath me was clouding my mind, just as I knew my proximity was clouding hers.

"I have never wanted you more than I do now, and I have never wanted anyone as much as I want you." I traced my lips over hers. She pushed forward to cement the kiss and I pulled back. Her baby-blues abruptly obscured behind a mist of betrayal and I didn't know if she was more hurt by my initial touch or the rejection of our almost kiss.

"I am not being fair. I want you and that is clouding your instincts." I quickly explained. The sting of rejection had pulled up her defences once more.

"You think too highly of yourself Trey. I do what I want, when I want," she said rigidly.

"And is this what you want? Five minutes after seeing each other for the first time in three years and you want to kiss as if nothing happened?" It was exactly what I wanted, but I knew Izzy better than that. She had too much stubborn pride to let that happen and not resent it, and I didn't want us to end up in a worse place than we currently were.

"No." She pouted adorably. I ran a finger across her jutted-out lower lip.

"Come down and watch tonight's gig. It's a warm up for the big one on Friday. I'd like for you to be there," I asked, almost begged.

"I don't know."

"It's up to you, but it would mean a lot to me. Oh, and here." I held out my room key. I knew Izzy would understand the significance. It was an invitation to strip me bare and know me in my entirety. She took the key with trembling fingers, appearing surprised that I was doing this, inviting her in. I nodded to reassure her then strode purposefully toward the door. She needed the space to think and so did I.

"Nothing is out of bounds to you. If you have questions, I will answer them all after the gig tonight. I know it is a long time coming and maybe it is even too late, but you deserve to know. *If* that is what you want." I was relieved to hear the words come out so calm and controlled because, for the first time in a long time, I was terrified. Nevertheless, I promised myself I would do this. I had lived the last three years in a twisted kind of limbo, running away from my fears whilst simultaneously sinking in them. At least by the end of this night, I would know where I stood.

FIVE.

~Izzy~

I sat on the sofa for way too long after Trey left. I was cold, tired, and hungry. I stank of accumulated sweat, fear and lust. I really needed a shower.

I turned the little key in my hand. Both bedrooms had locks on them, but when Trey and I started dating, I hadn't seen the point of locking my door. Whether he was in my room or his, it didn't matter, I trusted him in my space. I trusted him to look after me and keep me safe. It always hurt that he didn't return that trust. Until now.

My thoughts were fluttering wings in my head, each idea fighting for the right to fly. The moral decision of whether or not to accept his offer was the most dominant argument. I didn't know if I had any right to go through his things. Or if I even needed to.

I made a decision.

I wouldn't go in. His life was his own. How he lived it then and how he lived it now were his business. With the decision made my head eased a little but I needed a strategy. I needed some kind of plan that would help me keep it together around Trey. Admittedly, the anger of his betrayal had worn away ages ago. I came to realise that, although he shouldn't have lied to me, in a strange way he was trying to maintain the status quo between us. He cared about our relationship enough to protect what we had. Sure, he went about it all wrong but I came to understand it. Eventually.

After I let the worst of the hurt go, I found myself curious about his proclivities. My initial research unearthed unsavoury and completely untrue 'facts' across the web. Nevertheless, I tried again, determined that the man I knew wasn't the freak these idiots labelled him. Eventually I found a site and a few people who were willing to share their experiences with me and the more I learned, the more I wanted to learn. I wasn't brave enough to try anything out, mostly because I needed a trustworthy partner to experiment with. BDSM wasn't something I would enter into with a stranger and just cross my fingers that I woke up okay the next day. The whole nature of Dominance and submission was based on trust. I trusted no one more than I trusted Trey and therein lay my dilemma. For the longest time I wanted him back. I wanted to turn back the clock and relive that awful day all over again knowing what I know now.

I figured Trey's serendipitous return was my chance. If we could talk things through, sort them out and move forward, perhaps we could try again. If he still wanted me, of course.

I looked at the key in my hand. This proved it, didn't it? Why let me into his life if he didn't want me to be a long-term part of it? The real question was in what capacity would I remain? Friend? Lover? Sub?

I was getting ahead of myself. Firstly, I needed to shower then find clothes suitable for the club, something sexy and eye catching. I wanted to make him desire me. I would go to his set tonight and then give him the opportunity to talk later.

After that, it was out of my hands.

SIX.

The club was heaving. Despite this being a private show, there were at least a hundred people piled into the tight backroom. Sam's club was split by a clever folding wall, which allowed her to divide the huge space into two smaller areas during weeknights, or open it up into one large space on weekends. Not only did it mean she could host a public bar and private functions simultaneously but that she could handle live music during the week nights while still keeping her regulars happy out in the front bar.

The bar was how I met her way back when I first left university. I saw a sloppy bit of cardboard pressed up against the street-side window. It read *'Help wanted. Ask inside for Sam.'* I sauntered inside, feeling bold, and bounced myself up onto a barstool. I waited for the broad-shouldered, brown-haired, tasty bit of flesh behind the bar to turn around and notice me.

"You know we are closed, right, Short-stuff?" he said without turning around.

"Your door is open and the sign said to ask about the job, so here I am."

"You're here about the bar work? Have you ever tended bar before?"

"No, but I am a quick learner and I need the cash."

"We don't pay much."

"I don't mind. I lose my apartment next week and if I don't get something soon I am going to have to sleep on the street. You wouldn't want to do that to a poor little thing like me would you, Sam?"

The hunk eyed me with unveiled curiosity. "Hmm emotional blackmail won't win you any points with me, Short-stuff."

"Really? Heartless are you? Well, what else can I possibly offer a handsome man like you to secure the job?" I teased, totally out of my depth but desperate. He laughed at me, his great booming laugh rattled the bottles behind the bar.

"Hey Sam!" He yelled, tilting his head towards the storeroom behind the bar. "I think we might have found a new barmaid."

"What's that? You've finally found one you like, Trey?" A female voice yelled back as she made her way into the bar.

"She's got more spunk than the other graduates that fall through the door," he returned, still looking at me.

"Not yet I've not, but that sounds like fun," I mumbled quietly, although not quietly enough because Trey looked up, cocked a single brow, and grinned.

"Hi there!" Sam smiled, offering me her hand across the wide mahogany bar. "I am Samantha James, I'm the owner of the bar and employer of this miscreant. Why don't you come through to the office and we can talk properly." And that was it. I got the job. Later, when I lost my university accommodation, I moved into the apartment above the bar with Trey.

The bar hadn't changed in all the years between. The live bands that played here over the years kept it contemporary. The club had become an unofficial Mecca for bands and record labels alike. You knew if you played here, you had either made it or were about to. Sam hadn't picked a bad band yet.

The folding wall was closed tonight. Sam played hostess, flitting between the two zones and shaking hands with people more suited to desk-work than a metal gig. The agents were all in tonight. It looked good for Trey and the band.

"You going through or what?" A familiar voice whispered in my ear. "You won't be able to watch me air-fuck you from here, Cutie."

"Xadian!" I exhaled his name on a happy breath. I hadn't realised how badly I had missed the other band members until Xade's familiar scent washed across me. They had been like brothers to me, but they were loyal to Trey and for that reason alone I hadn't seen hide nor hair of them in three years.

"It is good to see you again, Izzy,"

"You too, Xade."

"So are you coming through?"

"Yeah. I just needed a little Dutch courage first."

"Well drink up because we're on in five."

"Then why are you out front? Shouldn't you be getting in the zone or something?"

"I was looking for someone."

"Oh yeah?"

"But it looks like she wasn't as brave as you." He glanced around the space once more before a little glimmer of hope faded from his eyes. Xade took a deep breath and let it out in a whoosh of air. "Oh well. He loves you, you know. He might not have said it, but he does. The last three years have eaten at him. I know that's not your concern. He fucked up, I get that, but he has suffered for it too. Hear him out, yeah? Even if it is just to bring you both closure. You both need that to move on."

"I know. I will."

"Glad to hear it. We all fuck up sometimes. Some of us worse than others. It's how you make up for the mistakes that counts. Well, I will see you out there." He raised a hand in mock salute and sneaked in behind the bar, heading towards the offices and backstage area. It bugged me to see him so hurt and not know what made him that way but anything could have gone down in the last three years and I wouldn't know.

I ordered a few more drinks before I mustered the courage to step through the divide. Sam glanced up at me from her seat by the door. She sat with the suits in one of the booths lining the walls. I nodded to her and then disappeared into the crowd. I kept myself close to the back and leaned against the cool panels of the folding wall. The band were already most of the way through the set. I had missed the majority of their performance. Regretfully, I watched as they got ready for their final track of the night.

The crowd cheered and catcalled as Trey stepped up with an acoustic guitar. To my surprise, Trey took to the mic and, without the backing of the band, began to sing. It was a ballad, but it was not the departure from their usual sound that had me hyperventilating, it was the lyrics.

That day embedded in my brain
Burrows like poison through my aching heart
The day you walked in on me with her
And I shattered us apart.
I never meant to break you.
I never meant to make you cry.
I never wanted to drive you
Into the arms of some other guy
But I fucked it up
I put my needs before you
because, Angel, I just never knew
That all I ever needed was you.

Every day since has been a fight
Running from the pain, I caused you.
Praying for the chance to make it right
But I was too afraid to ask you to stay.
I never meant to break you.
I never meant to make you cry.
I never wanted to leave you
Or for us to have to say goodbye.
But I fucked it up

And I never got the chance to say
That, Angel, when I broke you,
I broke me too.
Oh Angel, it broke me too.

I struggled to see him through a veil of tears, but I knew he was looking right at me. People turned to stare. Some cooed and others glared. I didn't care about them or what they thought.

"I know you didn't use the key. You wouldn't. Go. Do it now, Angel. Take it all out and lay it out for us. This time I'm not leaving until I make it right." Trey's silken voice touched me through the crowd. On trembling legs, I staggered to the exit. Sam offered me an encouraging smile as I passed her. I smiled weakly back. I hurried through the front bar and out into the cool night air.

I needed to breathe. I needed a second to compose myself and not let Trey sweep me off my feet with one song. I tried to remind myself that he wasn't asking for a way back. He was only promising to fix the damage. Did he realise that it wouldn't be enough? That the only way I would be fixed was to have him be mine or be rid of him for good? This half-life, living without him and still expecting him to come home to his room, his stuff, his bed, was killing me.

The cold air slammed against me, pushing me further into the glass wall of the club.

I tugged my phone from my pocket and called Kye.

"What do you want?" His tone was biting but I needed him. I swallowed my guilt. I swallowed my annoyance too.

"Trey has apologised. He wants me to meet him. We are going to go through everything." I spluttered. My words tumbled out too fast but Kye heard me clearly.

"Shit. Is that what you want?"

"Yes. No. I don't know."

"Izzy, be sure. I can't watch you go through that again."

"I love him. I always have. I want him back and you know I'm okay with his lifestyle. It's just—"

"What?"

"Am I doing the right thing? Am I making it too easy on him? Does it make me weak that I want him back?"

"Oh Izzy! Weak? You are the most stubborn idiot I know. You spent three years without him despite having forgiven him in the first week of being apart. You refused to track him down. You tried to move on. I think you have punished both of you enough for his mistake. If you can see past what he did, and you can learn to trust him again, then fuck what anyone else thinks."

"He still needs to learn a few things about being in a relationship."

"No kidding, but if you don't make the effort to teach him then how is he going to learn? Listen, Izzy, you know you need to give it a second chance. If you don't you will regret it, but don't just accept him because he apologises and then expect everything to go back to the way it was. Nothing is the same the second time around. If you go for it again, do it on your terms. No one needs to take shit in their lives no matter how lonely it gets sometimes." His words were harsh but his tone soft.

"Thanks, Kye."

"Will you be okay?"

"Yeah."

"Good luck and I am still pissed with you but call me in the morning to tell me how it went anyway."

"I will," I replied but he had already gone.

His words stuck with me. If I wanted a second chance, it was up to me to ensure it happened on my terms. With my mind made up, I slipped into the apartment and cleared out my bedside cabinet.

SEVEN.

~Trey~

It took too fucking long for us to pack up and get the hell out of the bar. I tried to slip away a couple of times but each time I did, another agent, promoter or crazy fan stepped in my way and kept me chatting. Hadn't they heard me out there tonight? Didn't they realise that I had shit to do?

"Xade, I gotta go, do you think you can handle this? I can't be here any longer. She has waited long enough and so have I," I shamelessly begged my best friend.

"Sure, we won't make any decisions tonight anyway. You go on ahead. I will arrange something back at the hotel if you need to find us. If things work out, bring Izzy too."

"Thanks man."

I rushed out and around to the back of the building where a small black door waited for my key. I pulled the ring out and found the right key, then slipped it into the lock, sucking in a harsh breath as it turned. I shoved myself up the narrow staircase and in through the second doorway. I expected to see her on the couch or at the counter in the kitchen area, but the spaces were both dark and deserted. My anger and disappointment flooded into my chest. I was too late. She had gone again.

I walked down the corridor toward her room, however, that too had been abandoned. My fists clenched until they hurt and the voice in my head screamed at me to punch something. I couldn't believe that I had lost her again. The song must have been too much or maybe she came back here, looked at my playthings, and decided I wasn't what she wanted? I didn't know and the possibilities were ringing in my ears until I heard her tiny breaths, in and out, coming from my room. My feet carried me there like wings. I didn't feel the footfalls on the old wooden boards.

My door swung open and before me was such an unexpected sight that I felt sure I was hallucinating it.

"Trey, baby, look at me," Izzy whispered gently to me. I stopped my frantic search for an explanation as if something in the room, other than Izzy, could give it to me.

"I…I can't…" I stuttered on trembling breath.

"You can. You can look and take in the scene, or would you like me to explain it to you?"

"But you are…you—"

"Trey. Just describe what you see, Baby." I couldn't describe it. I dreamed of this a thousand times and yet now that she was before me, *like this*, I just couldn't accept it. My beautiful little angel was on her knees in a perfect submissive position. She wore nothing but a red ribbon at her throat and nipple clamps connected by a heavy chain. Her stiffened, aching nipples wore it proudly. My cock jumped, reminding me of its existence. It took me a second to remember how to speak, but I had already forgotten whatever it was she said.

"You are beautiful and this is a mistake." I reached out for Izzy and tried to pull her to her feet. She took my hand and squeezed it gently, causing the chain to sway and her beautiful breasts to tremor. I forgot everything again.

"Trey? Is everything okay?" She asked, snapping me out of my stupor.

"Yeah. No." She tilted her head and watched me. Her amusement tugged at her lip and drew out a smirk. "Izzy, I don't want you to do this for me. I don't want you to pretend that this is what you want, because you will grow to despise me and yourself. This isn't something you can just fake." I said as gently as possible. I appreciated what she was trying to offer but she didn't know what she was getting into.

"There you go again, Trey. Assuming too much." She laughed.

"What do you mean?"

"Have you ever asked me what I thought about all of this?" She asked, waving her hands and indicating the array of objects she had lovingly laid out on my bed. I shook my head, not daring to believe what she might be saying.

"Fucking hell, Trey. Take a look. Does any of that stuff even seem familiar to you?" She asked and I looked around, attempting to understand what she was saying. The objects were not mine. I took three long strides to my tallboy and pulled open the top drawer.

Inside, still arranged in my ultra-neat fashion, were my playthings. I looked over to the corner and, yes, there stood my trunk. Unopened.

"These are yours?" Izzy nodded in response. "You never said."

"I didn't know until you had gone. I was curious and that curiosity became more."

"Have you...are you..." I was unsure how to ask if she was with someone else. If she had given herself to another Dominant but she understood my meaning.

"I have been waiting for you," she admitted and her words lit up my world.

"I was hoping you would say that." Dropping to my knees in front of her, the smell of cigarettes, booze and sweat saturating the air around us, I reached for Izzy's hair. With the softest of tugs I arched her head back. She smirked again.

"I can take it harder you know." She teased. I kissed her. My hot breath invaded her mouth. I tasted her fruity flavour and groaned out my contentment. I missed her.

"I bet you can, Baby." She made a cute little *'mmm hmm'* sound of agreement that just encouraged me to kiss her again. When she was breathless and I was in a similar state, I asked her another question.

"Do you know what I am?"

"Yes," she purred. "A Dom."

"That's right and do you know what that will make you?"

"Your sub."

"Two for two, Baby. So, you should know that it is my job to take care of you. To give you what you need, even if it sometimes isn't what you think you want. I make decisions for you, baby, and you have to trust that I am always going to act in your best interest. I will never harm you. It will always be safe and consensual. There will be rules that we both have to agree to."

"I understand. I want that. I want to please you. To pleasure you in every way you need. I know that I will get the same in return." Her response was determined. Fierce. I almost laughed at the completely unsubmissive way she had been behaving since I walked in the room. She was unconsciously topping at every turn, but we had plenty of time to learn together.

"Good. Now get yourself up on that bed, Izzy. We can play another night. Right now I just want to be inside you." She looked confused, a sweet combination of disappointment and relief crossed her face. I didn't let it linger there for long. Divesting myself of my clothing, I climbed over her, propping myself up on my elbows. I ran a single digit down her cheek, across the hollow at her throat and down the valley between her heaving breasts. I caught the chain between my finger and thumb and pulled it gently. Both nipples extended up and gravitated together. Izzy sucked in a sharp breath.

"Have you played with this before?" I asked curiously. She nodded, her body shivered with each small movement of the chain. She used a beginner's clamp. Tweezer-like ends pinched the nipples in a sweet nip. I was pleased she hadn't mistakenly used something that might have caused her harm. A larger hoop in the centre of the chain indicated that a third clamp had been removed. I flicked again, causing Izzy to groan appreciatively. "Where is the missing chain, Angel?"

"You're seriously asking that right now?" She griped. Instinct overtook me. I had her flipped onto all fours before she could blink and brought my palm down upon her cheek. I was gentle but she hissed. I pressed myself to her back and moved my lips across her earlobe. "You okay, Baby? Is this still what you want? Just say no and we stop."

"Yes. Oh God yes. That was good Trey." She virtually vibrated beneath me.

"Where is it then? And mind your manners, Angel."

"My bag. On the floor."

I reached down and found the little pink bag. In one of the compartments was the chain I was looking for. Lubes, gels, condoms and a variety of vibrators were neatly arranged in the other sections. My angel came prepared. I took what I needed and climbed up behind her. Using my left hand, I caressed her back in circles, whilst my right reached underneath and clipped the chain to the loop. Running my fingers along the dangling chain, I grasped the clamp end and warmed it in my clenched fist.

Izzy held her body taut. I queried her trepidation. "You haven't tried this end?"

"No. I wasn't sure if I could –"

"You didn't think you could handle the sensation of it gripping your clit?" I guessed. Her nod confirmed my suspicion.

"Do you trust me when I say not only can you handle it, but you are going to come quick and hard from it?"

"Yes," she said eagerly. "I trust you and I believe you."

"Good girl."

I ran it teasingly along her hot wet slit, coating it in her essence and then clipped it to her swollen bud with a practiced hand. Izzy squeaked at the pinch. I held her steady with one hand whilst still gripping the chain. I wanted her to grow accustomed to the compression before I added any more stimulation. When I let go she was going to feel the pull of gravity on the heavy chain.

"Okay?" I asked. She hummed. I slowly released the chain, ensuring that it remained still. I only wanted her to feel the pull not the swing.

"Oh, oh God! That's—"

"Good?"

"Yes. Oh yes, good," she moaned. I chuckled.

"In a moment I am going to slip my cock inside you, Angel," I said as I slipped two fingers inside her weeping pussy. I pumped them slowly, still holding her still with my hand on her back. "You are good and wet, but I need you to tell me that you want it."

"Trey, I do. I want you. God please hurry up. I need you."

I removed my fingers from her and fisted my cock, coating myself in her, sliding her slickness over me. One, two, three pumps and I positioned myself. One deep breath and I pushed inside. The heat. The intense heat of her cunt was delicious. My slow entry ached. The desire to drive into her hard and fast was overwhelming

223

but my need to tease her was stronger. My second thrust pressed my pelvis deep into her round ass. My third slammed my balls against her with a decadent slap. The chain swung with every thrust. Her nipples and clit tugged with every back and forth motion.

I pulled her upwards so that we knelt together, her back tucked into my chest as I drove into her relentlessly. Her grunts and sighs were nourishment. I devoured them within kisses, my hand firmly holding her face so that I could watch every expression as it crossed her face. Her eyes rolled back, the lids fluttered then Izzy uttered a beautiful high-pitched shriek. It was an animalistic song of pleasure that split my chest open with pride. That she wanted me, trusted me, and came beneath me, was all I ever wanted. It was more than I could have hoped for.

She came hard and fast, liked I promised she would, my own release spurting not long after hers. We lay, sated and spent, together on my bed. I gently released the single clamp that had managed to remain on and eased the pressure at her nipple with my finger. I had ointment, I needed to get it for her, but when I tried to stand, she grabbed my wrist and pulled me back to her.

"Why didn't you want to do more? Was that enough for you? Did it sate your," she trembled and blushed, "needs?"

I guessed at her fears. She said something before about not being woman enough for me. Didn't she realise she was more that I ever dreamed of having? To stop her worrying I explained myself. "You have no idea how I have missed you. Just you," I began. "When I broke us, I spent a long time trying to piece myself back together but nothing I did worked. Nothing helped, not the band, not the music - nothing. It took me a long time to realise what was wrong. You see I couldn't put myself back together, Izzy, because the most important piece of me was missing. I left it behind." I kissed away the tears that fell from her eyes. I never wanted to make her cry again but these were tears of understanding and happiness. I fed her with kisses, each one punctuating the truth of my confession, "And now I have you. I am whole again. Izzy, my angel, how could you not know? The best piece of me was always, inevitably, you."

HE SAID YES

By Felicia Fox

I felt the back of my earring slip from my fingers. "Damn it!"

I looked to my husband, Aaron. His five-foot-ten form was sitting on the bed, bent over at the waist slipping on his black leather dress shoes. He looked over at me and his face softened. I was a mess of nerves and I'm sure helplessness was written all over me.

I focused on a little patch of his jet black hair on his head. His cowlick always stuck out, even a little bit and I wanted to smooth it. Not because it was out of place but because it was incredibly adorable. Right now looking at that cowlick was better than looking into his face and seeing compassionate eyes.

"What's wrong, baby?"

"I dropped the back of my earring," I griped and then fell to my knees to find the little gold backing. Frantically my hands rubbed over the carpet to feel for the small metal piece.

"I know you're nervous, Crista, but what I don't understand is why. Talk to me."

I found the back and turned away to answer him. "I'm afraid you'll look at me differently or that you will be jealous. I need you to understand that you are, and will always be, number one. I just don't want one night to mess up what we have now." I turned back to face him when the last word left my mouth.

I stood in the night's lingerie, a strapless black satin bra with the panties to match. I felt like I needed to be wearing more clothing to armor me to whatever words he might say next. *Way to be a pessimist Crista.*

"I know that Crista. It's why I am okay with all of this. Your fear for my reaction is enough to let me know that how I feel means more to you than adding a little extra fun to our night."

"Are you sure? Knowing about my past and actually seeing it—"

"Please, stop asking, because if you're this worried I don't think we should go through with it."

He was being so much more patient with me than I would have been with him. I took a deep breath to calm my nerves and managed a shaky smile.

"I'm okay, I promise. I just needed to know you were, too."

Aaron stood and walked over to me. His steps were sure and his intentions clear. The look in his eyes said he was going to devour me. I shivered in expectation. His arms entwined around me and my hands settled on his shoulders. His face leaned in and I sighed in happy relief.

It was, at first, a soft meeting of lips that slowly increased with each movement. Aaron's hands were balled against the small of my back holding me tight to him. I could feel the hard plains of his chest that I knew came from time spent at the gym.

"God I love you." I panted, when his hands moved from my lower back to grip my ass firmly.

Aaron's tongue snaked out to dance with mine as my mouth opened in a low and throaty whimper. "I love you too Crista. Now, are you ready?"

"I am."

"Well let's get going before I change my mind and fuck you here and now against the wall."

"I'm all for that option, too."

"Well then, how about a taste."

I giggled at his suggestion till I felt his fingers pull the fabric of my panties to the side. He glided against the lips of my sex. My pussy clenched wanting to be filled by his fingers. My sweet Aaron has always known just how to tease me. How to work me up with a few well placed touches and whispered words.

My hands clutched on to his shoulders fingers digging in to wrinkle the crisp white button down shirt he wore. "This pussy is mine, Crista and tonight we are going to play."

He pushed a thick masculine finger inside of my clenching sex. He pumped only a few times before pulling the digit out. I watched the arousal drip down. He eyed his finger in hunger until he placed it inside his mouth and sucked.

"Oh god, Aaron." I groaned and he covered my mouth with his own. I tasted myself and was revved to have him fuck me there and then.

"Good girl. Now let's get going."

He set me down on shaky legs. I leaned against the chest of drawers to settle myself. *God...* Even after all these years that man

228

has the ability to make my knees weak and my heart pound erratically in my chest. I was pretty sure that if my ribs hadn't caged it, my heart would have grown wings and taken flight with the abundance of love I have for my husband. I guess the greater challenge of tonight will be him still believing it when my body made love to another.

***

The lighting was dim where I sat waiting. The amber liquid swished around in the squat, thick-glassed tumbler. I sipped it, sucking air in between my teeth as the burn of it traveled over my tongue and down my throat to warm my belly. Soft music filtered in through the light chatter and clinking of glasses. I tapped my black stiletto to the unmistakable melody. My phone in hand, I once again looked at the time.

I was nervous and excited for the evening ahead. I grabbed a few strands of my long, brunette hair and twirled them. A bad habit from my youth, I was surprised I didn't have a bald spot because of it. *Should have worn my hair up.*

Little details spun around in my head on a loop. *Was what I was wearing okay?* It's not like there was a dress code for what I had planned this night. Still, I wanted to be enticing so I chose a strapless, black silk dress. I had to starve all day to fit into the sexy little number comfortably but it was worth it.

A hand slowly grazed the exposed skin of my back. I only knew of one person who touched me in that way. She was the woman I was waiting for this evening, Jilly. I shivered as her nails softly scrapped over my spine.

"I heard you like to be licked. Is this true?" The voice was feminine, low, and sultry. Her tone sent me reeling into a past where we were once inseparable.

I tried to turn so I could see her face but her hands gripped on to my arms from behind. Looking down, I saw her champagne colored nails. A definite contrast against the ivory of my skin. Images assaulted my mind of those same lightly, olive toned fingers running the length of my body. The memory of them pushing in between the swollen lips of my pussy had my breath coming in shallow pants.

A sudden surge of insecurities reared their ugly head for a second. *What if I'm not enough for her? My body has changed so much.*

It had been years since my head was in between the thighs of this woman. Twelve years to be exact. *What if I forgot how to be with a woman?*

The night before I became Mrs. Crista Marie Cota was the last. My best friend and maid of honor, Jillian, decided we should get drunk and fuck until the sun came up. She said I owed it to her for making her wear such a hideous dress.

Like Jillian would look awful in anything. She was a head shorter than my five-eight. With a come-fuck-me, hazel gaze and curves, she didn't have to try hard to convince me. To this day I could close my eyes and picture Jilly while Aaron had his mouth on me. He would suck and lick at the sweet cream of my arousal and I would bite my inner cheek to stop myself from calling out her name.

Jillian was a rockstar at giving face. Her tongue and fingers were magical. We played with each other off and on from high school through college and up until that last night together.

We had had an 'in the meantime' relationship. We fucked while in between boyfriends or just to scratch an itch when we were first learning about our sexuality. It had truly grown into an odd arrangement but it worked for us. We loved each other as friends and lovers but we both knew we needed more.

I ended up being the first to get married and I walked down the aisle with her scent still in my nose. I was almost scared to kiss my husband for fear that he might taste Jillian's juices on my lips.

Tonight was our anniversary and I wanted to give Aaron something he fantasized about. Aaron and I were both open with our sexuality. I even told him about Jillian. Not about the night before the wedding. That night was mine and I wasn't sharing that memory. Since then he salivated for a taste of what it would be like.

I still saw Jillian a few times a month and for family gatherings. She was married with two children of her own. Whenever we were all together my husband would wink at me like some horny teenager. It was both incredibly annoying and incredibly sexy. I, on the other hand, would have to check myself from looking at her longingly. My fingers would vibrate at the ghosted memory of what her flesh felt like against them. The way her body shuddered under my tongue made me clench my thighs.

"Are you sure you want to do this, Jilly? I don't want to be the cause of any problems between you and Marshal." I asked, giving her an out if she needed it.

"Crissy Cat," her voice was a little exasperated, I'm sure from the numerous times in the last week that I gave her the option to bail. "We have a deal. I come spend an evening with you and Aaron and you come with me and Marshal."

"I want to look at you Jilly. Let me look at you." I pleaded. I wanted to see her face. I needed the reassurance that she was really here. That I was going to touch her again after so long. She released my arms, her fingers glided over my skin causing goosebumps that I knew she could feel. I turned in my seat to look at her. The height of the bar stool put me at eye level with her.

Jilly wore her glossy, chestnut-colored hair down. Only mascara lengthened her eye lashes. Her natural beauty far out shined any need for heavy makeup. My hand snuck back up to twirl around the strands of my hair again.

"Crissy why are you so nervous? I can see it in your beautiful chocolate eyes."

"I...just...I'm ready," I stuttered over my words, all because she called my eyes beautiful. I needed to get a grip.

"Let's go then," she said gently.

I grabbed my purse and we both walked out of the bar. Luckily for me the bar was inside of the hotel we decided to stay in for the night. I might have chickened out had we needed to drive back to my house.

My stomach churned from anxiety. I wasn't scared about being with both Jilly and Aaron together. I feared that my feelings for her would be exposed. Laid bare before both of them in the way I looked at and touched her.

Waiting in front of the elevator I stared at the marble under my feet. My eyes followed the black veining of the tile as if it were the most interesting piece of news to hit main-stream media. The elevator dinged and we moved to get on. Elevators always made me nervous.

Stepping on to the floor of the damn death box, I felt a dip in my stomach. I gripped the side bar and heard Jillian giggle.

I looked up at her in mock irritation as the elevator's door closed. Instead of the usual eye roll she would dish out, she moved closer to me.

"I want you Crissy. I've missed your taste." Her voice was a whisper but in the quiet of the small space it felt magnified. Vibrating every nerve ending inside my body I held on to the hand-rail for support. My skin goose bumped and my nipples beaded.

Jilly stood so close, heat radiated off her in seductive waves. I wanted to rub my body against her like a purring kitten. Thoughts of relishing in the give of her soft curves had my thighs clenching together. The need to throw her down on the floor and fuck her was potent. I yanked myself back from the thought as I remembered that this was going to be an experience I was sharing with Aaron as well.

Our hands brushed up against each other with the lurch in the elevator as it began its ascent. My breath caught in the back of my throat. I looked down at her and found her face was already looking toward me. Her eyes were searching mine. It reminded me of the first time we ever touched. The budding arousal of youth made just the graze of her hand against any part of me a sensual delight. At the time I didn't have the reference of mind to understand. I did now though and it was delicious.

"Jilly—" I said breathless, but she cut me off before I could finish what I was about to say.

"Shh, Crissy." We both leaned toward each other. The space between my lips and hers was just a hair's width apart. Her breath was warm against my lips. That small sliver of space was filled with so much anticipation and memories that I whimpered. I was so weak with need, I was afraid my knees would give and I would have to be carted out on a stretcher.

The elevator came to a stop rocking me away from her. I wanted to curse the timing. The doors opened and I pulled her along with me. I turned my head so I could look at her one more time. Her eyes were full of hunger.

I let go of her hand and fished the room's keycard out of my bag. Slipping it into the door I watched as the little indicator light clicked green. I took a deep breath and pushed the door open. Aaron sat in the chair he stationed on the side of the bed. The lighting was dimmed and I couldn't clearly see Aaron's expression.

He watched me enter and instead of getting up and walking over to greet us he remained seated. I heard the clink of ice. I gazed at his silhouette as he brought a glass to his lips. We discussed beforehand what he wanted from this. He wanted to watch until he couldn't help but touch.

Well my man wants a show. I will give it to him.

I set my purse down on the floor where I stood. Turning to face Jilly I pushed her hard up against the wall just as she closed the door behind her. Every emotion I had pent up inside of me surely smoldered in my gaze.

Jilly looked up at me through heavy lidded eyes. My hand moved up to her neck lightly and I could feel her pulse thud against the tips of my fingers. The blood pounded hard and fast. I smirked remembering how much she enjoyed my rough play. So I squeezed until her heartbeat had become erratic under my fingers.

Aaron was a very dominant lover and I luxuriated in submitting to him but there was just something about Jilly that made me demand her compliance. I craved her submission. The word "mine" repeatedly pounded in my head with every beat of her pulse against my hand.

Jilly gasped for what little air my hand allowed her to take in. Her lips were just slightly parted and I wanted to slam my mouth against hers. Her eyes slipped shut as she seemed to savor the feeling. Slowly my lips descended on hers. With the first touch I shivered. It was like coming home from a long trip, warm and welcomed.

The soft give of her pouty, pink mouth was delicious. I sunk my teeth into her lush bottom lip and she moaned against me. The deep sound traveled in a flash to my core. My sex soaked wet from her reaction. If not for my panties, my thighs would have been sticky with my arousal.

I wound my hands into her hair and pulled her head back sharply. Her lips parted wider on a groan and I slipped my tongue inside. She tasted of her favorite fruity gum. The same one she used to chew before we would fuck when we were younger.

I twined my tongue around hers deeply. Taking, owning, dominating her mouth was my mission. Her hands found my hips and she squeezed. I sucked on her bottom lip playfully and pulled away. Looking down, I watched her open, lust-glazed eyes and I was ready to make her mine again for one more night.

We moved to stand at the end of the bed. Slowly I descended to my knees. Lucky for me she had worn a dress too. The fabric hugged all her luscious curves and I relished pushing it up her open thighs.

Jesus help me! I saw she wore no panties. She had a lovely trimmed thatch of hair. I leaned my face into her and inhaled her musky scent. Her thighs trembled and I smiled. I raised my body from the ground. Pulling her dress up along the way my nails skimmed across her skin. I was so thankful for my height when I pulled the material off her with no hassle. I tossed the dress to the side, purposely making it land where I knew Aaron sat. He groaned letting me know how much he enjoyed watching.

The thought of his hand running the length of his cock, up and down while he watched me undress another woman emboldened me. I pushed Jilly back until she settled on to the bed. Her legs spread for me automatically.

In the little lighting we had I could see her sex glisten. My mouth watered for her taste on my tongue. My eyes went on a heated journey from her rounded hips to her full breasts, tipped with pretty raspberry colored nipples.

"You look hungry, Cris." Her voice was sultry and shot straight to my core.

"You're perfect, Jilly. I can't wait to have your taste in my mouth again." I watched as she writhed at my softly spoken words and my clit throbbed in need.

I moved, ready to crawl over her body and take one of those beaded peaks into my mouth when Aaron grabbed me from behind. His grip was firm and unrelenting and I had to swallow back an unexpected moan as I felt his warm flesh against my body. *When in the heck did he get undressed?*

"My sweet Crista," Aaron's deep masculine voice rolled over his tongue. "Jillian and I have a plan of our own." He whispered into my ear. The hair on the back of my neck stood and goose-bumps, once again, covered my arms. His length pressed into the small of my back and I panted. *What, in all that's holy, is going on?*

Aaron pinned my arms behind my back and I tried to wiggle to test his hold on me. He bit into the lower lobe of my ear as warning. "Be good." He whispered, his deep baritone voice making me shiver."

Jilly smiled and raised herself up slowly until she was in a seated position. Aaron leaned me forward and Jilly's arms wrapped around my body. Her fingers searched out the closures of my dress. I could feel the snick of the teeth on the zipper as she pulled the toggle down. Her movements were calculated. Her face was just inches away but I couldn't reach it with Aaron's hold on me.

The dress fell away from my body, gaining my full attention from the questions that raced in my head. A pile of black silk pooled around my feet. Jilly's hands were warm against my skin as she unclasped the back of my black strapless bra. She didn't seem impressed by my choice in lingerie. But when it came off and the creamy flesh of my breasts were exposed I saw the fire in her gaze. Her hands massaged roughly, pulling one breast toward her mouth. Heat enveloped the whole of my nipple and areola.

"That feels so good, Jilly." I whimpered as she sucked harder.

The hard thick length of my husband's cock was hot against my flesh. I moaned at the thought of him plunging himself into me while Jilly touched me. *When did they talk about this? How did I not know? It's not like either of them were any good at keeping a secret from me.*

"Fuck, Jilly." I moaned. The twin sensation of pleasure and pain as she twined her tongue around the pearled peak and then sunk her teeth was delightful.

"Do you like that, baby?" Aaron asked, "Does her mouth feel good on you? I bet it does but I think I need to find out for myself."

His teeth nipped at my neck while he subtly rocked his cock against me. Aaron's hand moved to my core. I felt him slide over the slight curve of my belly to the mound of my sex, his hand leaving a trail of fire against my skin.

I groaned as his fingers met with the silky hot juices he brought forth from me. His masculine fingers slipped through the lips of my pussy, circling my clit while Jilly licked and nibbled on both breasts.

"Oh god, yes!" I cried out.

Jilly's hands spread my pussy apart while Aaron played with my swollen and exposed clit. I could feel my arousal as it slipped from me. I was self-conscious for a second until her tongue followed the path from which it dripped, back up to my center.

"Jilly please don't stop." I pleaded. My body shuddered as she lapped at my pussy. Her tongue grazed the opening of my sex. Aaron's mouth was a constant sensation as his facial hair skimmed across the too sensitive skin of my shoulder and neck.

"You taste so good Cris, just like I remembered. Aaron you are so lucky." Jilly spoke low and directly into my pussy. I could feel her words vibrate between each warm, slick, slide of her tongue.

"I know Jillian. Why don't you share with me? Dip your fingers into her cunt and bring them to my mouth."

"As you wish." Jilly purred and I felt my knees go weak as two fingers pushed home. My pussy squeezed tight around her fingers as it clenched in need. It made her fingers feel full inside of me. In and out she stroked. Warmth spread from my groin into my belly and legs. Jilly removed her fingers and stood leaning her body into mine. Her soft flesh pushed seductively against mine.

"Taste, Aaron." She demanded of him. I kept my eyes locked on hers while the sound of my husband licking and sucking juices off Jilly's hand played an erotic tune in my ear.

"Please!" I whimpered, desperate for them to just take me already. Stop dragging it out. I wanted it and I wanted it now. I was not a patient woman.

"Not yet, Cris. I want to feel your mouth on my dick." He let me go and I dropped to my knees. Jilly and I were positioned on either side of his cock. I kept my eyes locked on hers even as I began to lower my mouth to the side of Aaron's hardened shaft.

Our tongues traced over the thick veins down his dick, each alternating our path up and down the length. I took Aaron's cock in my hand and licked and nibbled around the head and Jilly joined me in this sinful kiss. Our tongues met. Our hands pumped. Aaron thrusted his hips. I broke eye contact with Jilly and looked up at my husband. He was amazing with his head tilted back, the veins in his neck straining.

His hand wound in my hair and he pulled my head away. Leaning down his lips slanted over mine. His mouth tasted of mint and whiskey. He had a few days worth of stubble and I felt it brush roughly against my skin as he intensified the kiss.

"Oh Cris…Jilly's mouth. It. Feels. So good." Aaron moaned into my mouth before he pulled away. I looked back at his cock and saw Jilly's lips had wrapped around the crown of his shaft. Her cheeks hollowing as she sucked.

Aaron's hand tightened in my hair as Jilly increased her speed. She pulled away from him with a pop and I descended on his cock where she left off. I could taste Aaron's salty pre-come. He was delicious.

Jilly's hand crept up my thigh while Aaron's cock was in my mouth. Her fingers pushed between my swollen folds. I gasped and Aaron pushed his dick further in between my lips and I gagged but kept pace. Saliva dripped with each thrust of his cock, leaking onto my breasts.

"That's right, Cris. Suck your husband's cock. Take it deep." Jilly's commanding voice had me working Aaron's shaft even harder. My hand moved up and down the length in tandem with my mouth.

Aaron pulled me away from his cock by my hair, his grip at the nape of my neck lifted me into a standing position. "I love you baby." He growled against my lips before crushing his mouth against mine.

I felt the loss of Jilly's fingers as they slipped from my pussy. The arousal she was working from my core dripped down my thigh as Aaron pushed me away from him and down onto the bed.

Jilly straddled over my face. She looked down at me, her hazel eyes crashing with a wave of emotions into mine. In that moment I knew she felt the same way. She had been holding herself back just like I had been.

How the hell was I supposed to go back to the way things were after this? Will we have to avoid each other? Would our lives become awkward?

All thoughts drifted as I looked at her sex deliciously drenched for me. Suddenly I was so very ravenous to have her flavor on my tongue. I spread the lips of her pussy open and took a long swipe from the dip of her core to her clit. I collected her juice and savored the slide of it down my throat. She was sweet like honeydew with the tiniest tang. I inhaled deeply wanting to keep this new memory of her taste with me.

"Oh Crissy your tongue feels so good." Jilly groaned as she settled on my face, rocking herself from my nose to my chin. The drag of her pussy against my skin was so fucking hot. I gripped her ass tighter to move her more quickly. My tongue slipped inside of her and she pushed down harder. I teased her dripping cunt flicking my tongue inside her sex, "Oh fuck, Cris yes." Jilly's moans were so sexy.

She pulled herself away from my mouth, "Come back here." I whimpered, my hands trying to pull her back to my mouth

Aaron yanked me down the bed by my ankle. "My turn." He growled. Aaron spread my thighs open wide and glided his cock over my swollen bud, teasing me. I wanted to feel him ramming his steel hard shaft inside. I wanted to have Jilly's pussy back on my face, riding me. So much sensation, I didn't know where to start first. I just knew I was a greedy bitch and wanted it all.

242

The head of Aaron's dick pushed its way into my clenching cunt and I cried out, "Oh my fucking God, Aaron."

It was one long thrust until all eight, thick, inches were sheathed inside of me. My mouth opened in a moan and was immediately covered by Jilly's sweet lips over mine. She tasted like a sinful combination of my pussy and Aaron's cock. It was all of us together. Our tongues twined and the full feeling of Aaron deep inside of my pussy was decadent.

Jilly's hand moved to my neck just as Aaron pulled his cock out of me, until just the head of his dick was inside. Jilly's hand squeezed and Aaron slammed himself into my sex. It bordered on painful. I gripped the sheet under my body and the fabric twisted so tight in my hands I thought it might rip but I couldn't scream with Jilly's grip on my neck.

"You're so tight baby and when Jilly squeezes I can feel you clench harder around my cock." He punctuated the word cock with the hard thrust of his shaft into me.

Both Jilly and Aaron were in sync with one another. As he increased the speed of his thrusting, she would put more pressure around my neck. Her free hand moved to my clit, rubbing in torturously slow circles that had my back arching. I released my hold on the sheet and moved my hand to Jilly's core. The silky heat of her sex made me shiver. God how I wanted her back on my face riding me until she came all over my face.

My thoughts were foggy. I could feel sweat cover my body as I tried to take in what little air I was receiving from Jilly's mouth.

The dominance was a new side of her and I needed more of it. Aaron moved in deep one last time, holding himself inside my sopping wet sheath.

Jilly let go of my neck and moved away from the bed. Before I could cry about the loss of her touch Aaron bent over me, his lips wrapped around my nipple. He twirled his tongue over the budded peak and bit down just the way he knew I liked it.

"Mmm, yes! Oh god yes!" I cried out. Aaron had bit down hard enough to make me want to pull away but not hard enough to break skin. I would be sore tomorrow and every time my blouse or the lace of my bra rubbed I would remember exactly why they ached so deliciously.

"I know what my baby needs." He moved his mouth to the other nipple and did the same. I cried out even louder than I had before. Aaron soothed the sting over with his tongue then leaned up and kissed me sweetly on the forehead.

"You are such a good girl, Cris. I hope you're ready." He groaned to me and then pulled out.

I felt so much loss with neither of them touching me until I leaned up and took in the picture that stood at the end of the bed. Aaron was helping Jilly tighten a D-ring that rested on her hip. She was wearing a strap-on. I was at a loss for words until I saw her place her palm on his cheek. She raised her self on tip-toes and kissed his lips so softly, so full of emotion. One would think that I would have been jealous but instead I found it beautiful.

"Thank you." She spoke quietly to him and in response he winked and slapped her on the ass. *Ha! That's my man.*

Jilly climbed onto the bed next to me, "I've wanted to be with you again for so long. Come to me Crissy Cat." She pulled me on top. My legs were weak but I straddled her. As I lowered myself onto the dick she wore, the phallus stretched and filled me. I moaned and Jilly reached up to palm my breasts. She moved her hand and clicked something on the mound of the strap-on. My sex clenched as it began to vibrate. Her hands gripped tight on to my waist preventing me from jumping away from the intensity.

"Oh shit!" I called out and fell forward. My hands caught myself on either side of her head. I snapped my hips against hers, alternating with rotations.

"Fuck, Crissy. Mmm, this feels so fucking good." She groaned. The vibrations against her clit made her go crazy. I could see she was close and I wanted her to come for me. To watch her fall apart beneath me was lovely. It took me back to the days where her leg would be rested on one of my shoulders while I rubbed my pussy against hers until we spilled all over one another.

I felt as Aaron's oiled hand glided over my ass. He played with the puckered hole, rubbing until I relaxed, opening to him. He pushed his finger inside of me, readying my ass. I thought of how he would be pushing his cock deep inside of me instead of his finger and it made me moan. "Oh Aaron, yes. Please."

"Please what, Baby?"

"Fuck me."

"I will baby but I'm going to watch you squirm first."

"Move on me Cris, I need you, god I need you to move."
Jilly whimpered from under me as my pace lightened from the
distraction of Aaron playing with my ass. She reached up, grabbed
my face, and slammed her lips against mine. Her tongue moved in
and out of my mouth at the same steady movement as the cock she
moved in and out of my cunt. I felt a fresh wave of arousal flow
from me.

"Jilly yes, it feels so good. Don't stop. Please don't stop."

"I won't baby. Come on. Come for me. I can't hold on much
longer." Jilly replied and pushed up a harder making Aaron's finger
move in and out of me faster.

The side of the bed dipped and I looked over my shoulder. I
felt the head of Aaron's dick at my entrance as he positioned himself
to penetrate my ass. Slowly I rocked myself back on his length. The
vibrations and cock in my pussy had me on the edge of release. I
couldn't imagine what having his dick in me as well would do.

He pushed through that tight channel and I was full to
bursting with both Jilly and Aaron. Jilly was crying out as Aaron's
extra weight gave her the pressure she needed. She grew impatient
and pushed her hips up while Aaron pulled out a little. Both he and
Jilly moved inside of me alternately.

"Oh god! I can't! Oh god, this is too much," I cried out but
their paces only increased.

"You can do it Cris. You can take it for me, my love." Aaron
said punctuating the sentence with a smack to my ass.

Jilly whimpered under me and I looked down at her beautiful face. Her head was thrown back in surrender. "Crissy," Jillian chanted, and my heart lurched in my chest as she came undone beneath me.

Her pussy drenched the bed beneath us and her body twitched with each of Aaron's thrusts. She couldn't get away, being pinned down as she was. For a fleeting moment I felt cheated of her taste in my mouth. Those thoughts fled when her lips latched onto my breast. She sucked and nibbled around the mound.

Aaron continued his thrusting, moving me against the cock beneath me. "Oh god, Aaron! I'm there. So close, so close, so close baby." I pleaded.

Like flash paper, every single nerve in my body caught fire until I exploded in a shower of orgasmic sparks. My body trembled and was drenched in sweat. Aaron kept up his pounding into me and I couldn't keep myself up any longer.

The vibrations and the cocks still sliding in and out of me was enough to almost send me into a second orgasm. I didn't know if I could take another one without blacking out. I leaned down on top of Jilly and she entwined her hands into my hair. She kissed me the best she could while I whimpered in her mouth.

I came again, not as potent as the first time but enough to weaken me till I just fell across Jilly. The cock she wore slipped from my pussy and I shuddered as Aaron still pounded me from behind.

"Fuck baby, I'm coming." Aaron growled. I could feel his shaft growing harder in my ass as he stuttered in his movements. The pulsing of his dick inside me let me know he was coming. Aaron pulled out slowly and I could feel his seed drip down the crack of my ass and the lips of my pussy.

Aaron fell over us with a grunt and I heard the click of Jilly turning off the vibrator. I don't know how much time passed as we all dozed off. When my eyes opened I found myself wrapped around Jilly and Aaron's arm draped over the both of us. The soft snore of my husband sleeping filled the air. The sound was familiar and comforting. I pushed my back against him so I could feel even closer to him. My leg covered Jilly's and my arm held her close to me. I snuggled my face into her hair and inhaled her scent. Having both of them sandwich me after everything we just did together was surreal but it felt right.

Jilly grabbed my hand and I jumped slightly. I was unsure how she would react to my octopus like grip on her. She kissed my fingers and turned over to face me.

"This won't change our lives. Unless you want it to." Jilly whispered low.

"What do you mean Jilly bean?" I asked using an old nickname and she smiled.

"We can do our session with my husband and end it there or we can maybe have a girl's weekend once in awhile. I talked to Marshal and he is supportive."

"I would need to talk to Aaron and see how he feels about that. As much as I want to scream yes and fuck you again, he is first."

"Don't be upset but he and I already talked about it." Her tone was worried.

"I don't know if I should be upset that I wasn't included in this talk or thankful that I didn't have to pluck up the courage to ask."

"You kept asking me if I was sure I wanted to go through with this night. I was worried you would back out. I called Aaron and we talked."

"I am almost afraid of what he said."

"I said yes." I startled at his deep baritone voice not realizing the light snore in the room was gone.

"Yes?" I questioned.

"Yes." They both responded in tandem.

"Well, okay." I mumbled. Both of them each took a hand at the same time. We laid in the quiet of the room holding hands. It was sweet and safe and almost too good to be true. I didn't know how this new future of possibilities would play out but I promised myself right then not to let fear stand in the way of it.

Playful Vibes

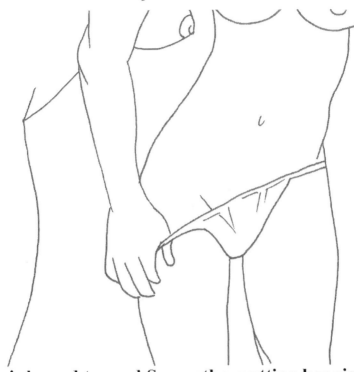

Alexis leaned toward Samantha, putting her right hand on her right inner thigh. Alexis firmly caressed her thigh as she moved her hand upward toward Samantha's tight little panties. Just as Alexis leaned in to kiss her, her hand finds Samantha's wet crotch. Kissing deeply, tongues grappling, while soft moans escape Samantha's mouth. Alexis then slipped a thumb through Samantha's panties and proceeded to gently pull them down as their lips touched once again. Their tongues twined together as Alexia pressed her hand firmly between Samantha's thighs.

Made in the USA
Lexington, KY
13 May 2015